Her mouth landed on his.

Sparks ignited, setting her veins on fire. She opened her mouth, her tongue playing with the seam of lips, plunging inside when they opened beneath her. Her arms twined his neck, her chest pressing into his as she tried to burrow closer, pull herself deeper into him.

A log fell in the fireplace with a loud crash. They broke apart at the sound. Finley looked up at Will from her under lashes. "Sorry, I didn't mean to break the truce."

"Don't apologize." Will's gaze reflected the flames dancing in the fireplace. His hands tightened on her waist. "I was a willing participant."

She licked her lips. They were swollen. She could still taste Will. "But you said in the paddock—"

"I'll ask what I asked this morning. Is this what you really want or is it another game?"

She was about to faint from want. Her knees were soft with it. Her arms ached. "We're not meant for ever after. But for tonight, I want this. I want you."

"Tonight." His mouth closed over hers.

* * *

Ever After Exes by Susannah Erwin
is part of the Titans of Tech series.

Dear Reader,

When I started to write *Cinderella Unmasked*, I thought that book would be the only appearance of Finley Smythe in the Titans of Tech series. Fun fact: Finley was originally a male character, but I have brothers of my own and wanted to include a brother-sister relationship. Finley then made a brief appearance in *Who's the Boss Now?*, and it quickly became evident she needed a story all her own!

Finley is a master of control and management. She excels at arranging events—and people—just to her liking. But what happens when control is taken away from her by a natural disaster and she's stranded—albeit on a very luxurious ranch—with Will Taylor, the man who broke her heart fifteen years ago? Will is the one person who saw through her external armor to the real her underneath...except when it mattered the most, leaving her determined never to let anyone else in again.

I had a lot of fun writing Finley and Will's second chance at love, and I hope you enjoy reading it! And please stay in touch. You can find me on Twitter, @SusannahErwin, on Facebook at SusannahErwinAuthor, on BookBub at @SusannahErwin or at my website, www.susannaherwin.com.

Happy reading!

xoxo

Susannah

SUSANNAH ERWIN

EVER AFTER EXES

HARLEQUIN
DESIRE

DESIRE™

ISBN-13: 978-1-335-73549-2

Ever After Exes

Copyright © 2022 by Susannah Erwin

Recycling programs
for this product may
not exist in your area.

This edition published by arrangement with Harlequin Books S.A.

For questions and comments about the quality of this book,
please contact us at CustomerService@Harlequin.com.

Harlequin Enterprises ULC
22 Adelaide St. West, 41st Floor
Toronto, Ontario M5H 4E3, Canada
www.Harlequin.com

Printed in U.S.A.

A former Hollywood studio executive who gladly traded in her high heels and corner office for yoga pants and the local coffee shop, **Susannah Erwin** loves writing about ambitious, strong-willed people who can't help falling in love—whether they want to or not. Her first novel won the Golden Heart™ award from Romance Writers of America, and she is hard at work at her next in her Northern California home. She would be over the moon if you signed up for her newsletter via www.susannaherwin.com.

Books by Susannah Erwin

Harlequin Desire

Titans of Tech

Wanted: Billionaire's Wife
Cinderella Unmasked
Who's the Boss Now?
Ever After Exes

Visit her Author Profile page at Harlequin.com, or susannaherwin.com, for more titles.

You can also find Susannah Erwin on Facebook, along with other Harlequin Desire authors, at Facebook.com/harlequindesireauthors!

For Alex B.

Hope I did Finley justice!
Thanks for being a smashing sister-in-law.

One

"I hate weddings," Finley Smythe grumbled to the groom, who happened to be her half brother and favorite person in the world. "But this one will be perfect." She pinned the boutonnière of white rose, red berries and silver eucalyptus leaves on the lapel of his black tuxedo and stepped back. "There. Impeccable. And the rest of the day will follow suit."

Grayson Monk nodded at his reflection in the mirror here in the room set aside at the Saint Isadore winery for the groom and his attendants, and then turned to face Finley. "Nelle and I can't thank you enough for taking on the wedding planning. Despite your newly announced aversion. Which I'm fascinated by. I know how much you like events featuring cake."

"I don't have a problem with the idea of marriage

per se." Finley crossed the room to find her corsage, the black satin skirt of her formal gown rustling. "If people want to legally tie themselves to another person and check the 'married' box on their taxes, that should be their prerogative."

She picked up the flowers. The straight pin hidden in the wrapped stems pricked her right index finger and she shook her hand out of reflex. A tiny drop of blood landed on the cream lace bodice of her dress. She stared down at it. The spot was nearly imperceptible. But it was a flaw on a day Finley swore would be flawless. "This is not an omen," she said under her breath. "Everything will indeed be impeccable."

"So why do you hate weddings?" Grayson asked, having moved on to straightening his tie in the mirror.

She carefully pinned the flowers to her gown. "I object to the baroque language that sets unrealistic, illogical expectations. Phrases like *true love* and *until death do you part* and *soul mates* should be outlawed." Especially *soul mates*. Finley knew from experience the concept was a fraud.

She looked up to find Grayson regarding her, his brown gaze unreadable. "I don't find the phrases unrealistic. Nor illogical."

"Well, you wouldn't, would you? Few people getting married do. Or they wouldn't get married." Finley shrugged. "Where are your other groomsmen? Shouldn't they be back from seating guests by now?"

"I asked for time alone with my best man."

"Or best person, as the case may be." She indicated herself.

"You always have been, in my opinion." Grayson smiled, then his expression sobered. "I didn't say this enough growing up, but thank you for always being there for me."

"Well, someone had to raise you after Mom died." Finley smirked at him.

"Since you're only twenty months older, I'm pretty sure we raised each other. Which is why I know this past year has been tough——"

She waved a hand, attempting to dismiss the sentimentality threatening to swamp the atmosphere. "Tough? Why? Just because my boss was found guilty of violating campaign finance laws and is currently serving time in a federal correctional facility and I'm out of a job? Pfft. Walk in the park."

"I know you're trying to make a joke," Grayson said, apparently undeterred from having a serious conversation. "And Barrett wasn't just your boss, he was your stepfather."

"And your full father, so if anyone had a difficult time, it was you. Not to mention your bride, whose family was destroyed by Barrett. But we don't need to compete in the Pity Olympics on your wedding day." She glanced at the clock on the wall. "If Luke and Evan don't show up soon, we'll have to pay the musicians overtime."

Grayson took her hands in his. She went still. She and Grayson were close, but they weren't a family that engaged in much physical affection. "I'm trying to tell you how much you mean to me. And to Nelle. By taking on the wedding planning, you allowed her to spend time with her father before he passed, and she is forever grateful. I hope one day we'll be the ones making jokes at your wedding when you're attempting to have a heartfelt exchange."

Finley snatched her hands back. "Why do people about to be married always want to drag their unmarried acquaintances with them into the deep end?" A knock on the door heralded rescue. "Come in," she called. "Especially if your job is to get Grayson out of my hair and in front of the altar."

Luke Dallas and Evan Fletcher crowded into the room, handsome in tuxedos, their smiles bright as they approached Grayson and engaged in the ritual round of handshakes and back thumps that occurred among close male friends. Not that she expected much support from the newcomers when it came to dismissing weddings as archaic social rituals. Luke was hopelessly besotted with his wife, Danica, and their baby daughter. Evan had earlier told Finley he was thrilled Grayson and Nelle were holding their wedding at Saint Isadore, the Napa winery owned by his fiancée, Marguerite Delacroix, because it would serve as a test run for his and Marguerite's own nuptials in a few months.

Finley sighed. Sometimes it seemed like she was the only rational person in the room. She clapped her hands, interrupting the men. "Are the guests in their seats?" she asked Luke and Evan.

"Yes, ma'am," Evan said with a grin.

"Good." She patted Grayson on the arm. "Let's get you married."

Even Finley had to admit Saint Isadore was a spectacular venue for a wedding. Most Napa Valley wineries were legally prohibited from holding weddings to protect the fertile land, but Saint Isadore, built in the late nineteenth century to resemble a Loire Valley castle, was grandfathered in. The ceremony was taking place on the expansive flagstone terrace that divided the wing of the castle that held the owner's residence from the larger section that contained the winery offices and operations. At one end of the terrace, a freestanding rose-and-ivy-covered trellis surrounded by chairs for guests served as the altar, while the other end of the terrace was set up for the dinner reception to follow. Later, the trellis would be replaced by a stage for one of Nelle's favorite Bay Area bands to perform, while the chairs would be cleared to create a dance floor. All was arrayed against a stunning backdrop of gently rolling hills marked by neat rows of grapevines. The vines were still bare, but a recent storm meant the entire countryside was covered in lush green vegetation.

Finley took her place next to Grayson under the trellis, making one last visual sweep to ensure nothing was out of place, no detail had been overlooked. Not a single mote of dust marred her vision. Even the weather cooperated, the February afternoon a temperate sixty-seven degrees without a cloud in the sky despite the forecast for additional rain later in the week.

The string quartet issued the first notes of "Here Comes the Bride" and Finley turned in unison with the guests to see Nelle at the top of the makeshift aisle. Her white lace and tulle gown made her appear like the fairy-tale princess the press had proclaimed her to be when she and Grayson first met. Nelle's and Grayson's gazes locked, and Finley knew the rest of the winery had ceased to exist for them. They only saw each other.

She exhaled a deep breath and her shoulders relaxed. While there were still several hurdles to get through before the night would be over, the main objective of the event would be accomplished: joining Nelle and Grayson in matrimony. She allowed her gaze to idly wander over the guests' faces before turning back to listen to the minister as he started his invocation—

She froze, her breathing stopped, her heartbeat paused.

The man in the third row—it couldn't be him. Why would he be here? He had no connection to Nelle or Grayson. He definitely wasn't on the guest list.

Her pulse returned, faster, sharper, and she closed her eyes to run through a quick, calming breathing exercise. It was just her mind playing tricks. She blamed the earlier conversation about *true love* and *until death do you part* for causing her subconscious to dredge up long-forgotten—and good riddance to them, too—memories.

She opened her eyes and flicked her gaze sideways, just to check, to reassure herself she was imagining things. The man in the third row—fifth seat from the left on the bride's side—stared back at her, his expression still with shock. She swallowed, attempting to work moisture into her suddenly dry mouth.

It *was* him. She wasn't making it up. Will Taylor was at the wedding.

Will Taylor, who'd taught her the concept of soul mates was a farce. Will, who'd destroyed any pretensions she once held about true love and relationships that were meant to be.

Will, who'd walked away without a backward glance fifteen years ago, tearing her into tiny shards with his parting words.

Somehow, she pivoted and faced the minister. Somehow, enough of the ceremony penetrated the fog that had suddenly enveloped her so she could hand over the rings at the right time. She even produced a smile—not a big one, but then she was better known for her smirk—when Nelle and Grayson were pronounced wife and husband, and she was able to forget Will enough to genuinely laugh and clap when Grayson swept Nelle into his arms for an exaggerated backward dip followed by a very prolonged kiss.

Then it was time for the wedding party to follow the bride and groom back up the aisle. Finley straightened her spine and held her chin high in the air. She would not look at him. She would not look at him. She would not—

Will's chair was empty.

Two

Come to California, his sister Lauren had said a week ago. *We can spend time together, have a few laughs...*

The last thing Will Taylor felt like doing was laughing. Not with the gut punch he'd just received. He had been so stunned, he sat through most of the ceremony unable to move, unhearing, unseeing, before leaving his seat to find an unused corner of the winery terrace in which to process what happened. Or rather, who happened.

Finley Smythe.

As beautiful as ever. Not that it came as a surprise. He hadn't followed her career—he wasn't keen on inflicting pain on himself—but occasionally he'd catch a glimpse of her as he scrolled through cable news channels or glanced at the photos accompanying a magazine article, standing behind her stepfather the congressman. And despite living in Chicago, far from Barrett Monk's district in California, he'd heard about Monk's fall from grace—who with access to the internet hadn't? He just didn't put the groom's last name together with the ex-congressman and thus Finley.

Her straight dark hair was shorter, her figure under her cream-and-black gown leaner than in his memories. But she still possessed her regal poise. Still radiated a magnetic charisma that drew all eyes to her even with a magazine-ready bride walking down the aisle.

As unobtainable and out of his reach as ever, as her brief but scathing glance let him know.

Will grabbed the first full glass he saw on a passing serving tray. He downed it, not caring about the contents. How was this possible? Of all the weddings in all the world, how did Lauren manage to be invited to one featuring Finley Smythe as one of the groom's attendants?

"Hey, I finally found you." His sister appeared at his side as if he had summoned her with his thoughts. "You disappeared rather fast. Feeling okay?"

He wasn't sure what he felt, but *okay* was not near the top of the list of the words to describe the emotions coursing through him. Still, he nodded. "I'm fine."

Lauren raised her eyebrows, her lips pursed. "Not buying it. Do you want to go back to the hotel?"

"Honest, I'm good." He beckoned to a nearby wait-staff member and exchanged his empty glass for a full one, taking a second one to hand to Lauren. "I'm drinking wine at a winery. What could be wrong?"

Lauren's expression didn't change. "If you didn't want to be here, you should have said something when I asked. Then I could've found someone else to be my plus-one. Someone who would be happy to be at one of the Bay Area's most exclusive social events."

He gave himself a mental shake. No need to let the appearance of an old flame mar the day. Even if the churning in his stomach made it clear the fires weren't as banked as he thought they were. He smiled at his sister. "I'm happy to be with you. Been too long since we've been in the same place."

"And whose fault is that?" She laughed when they both answered, "Mine."

Then she sobered. "I do appreciate you escorting me to the wedding when Reid couldn't make it." She glanced down at the shiny platinum band on the fourth finger of her left hand, next to a ring set with a diamond so big, Will was pretty sure it could be seen from the International Space Station.

He nodded. "Reid knows the bride, right?"

"And the groom, but Nelle works for a children's nonprofit and he's their key sponsor, so they talk often. Nelle and I have become friends over the past year and I really like her, but I was aware I wouldn't know anyone else here." Lauren threw him a glance from under her eyelashes. "Which is why I thought you would be the perfect person to take to the wedding, because these are your people. Y'know, wheelers and dealers and chief executive officers. The crème de la crème of the tech industry."

"They are not my people." And once upon a time, Finley made it clear he was not, and never would be, her person.

"Really." Lauren folded her arms over her chest. "Last time I looked, you were a tech CEO."

"EverAftr is based in Chicago, not Silicon Valley."

"So? Screenweb is building a reality TV series around you."

"They're building it around EverAftr. The idea is to follow people from all over the country as they look for their romantic partners."

"But you're the star of the first season."

"EverAftr is the subject of the entire series."

Lauren huffed, but humor twinkled in her eyes. "Fine. Pretend you're not wholly responsible for Ever-Aftr's success and the key reason why the company landed a TV deal."

Will's gaze zeroed in on Finley, despite the cheerful throng of guests crowding the winery's terrace between them. Most of the time, he thought his excellent recall was a gift. His memory wasn't eidetic—he couldn't amaze his friends by listing all the details of a meal he ate six years ago—but his mind was like an easily accessible filing cabinet stocked full of facts and figures as well as sounds, textures and sights. And right now, all he could remember was Finley.

The satin smoothness of her skin under his fingertips.

The dazzling light in her caramel-brown eyes when he made her laugh.

The soft gasp tickling his ear when he moved his mouth lower, to—

"Are you sure you're okay?" Lauren waved a hand in front of his face. "You haven't heard a word I've said. And your cheeks are flushed."

Will blinked and the memories disappeared, to be locked securely away this time. He hoped. "Just cold. The wind is picking up. I'm surprised the reception isn't being held indoors."

"You have to be kidding. It's a gorgeous day and there are patio heaters all over. If we stop hanging out in this corner and mingle with the other guests, you'll be toasty warm." Lauren indicated the trays of food being passed several feet away. "Besides, aren't you hungry? I heard the winery uses a three-star Michelin chef as their caterer."

His gaze sought Finley anew, a magnet he was powerless to resist. She was gathered with the rest of the wedding party, taking post-ceremony photos. The golden late afternoon sun created a halo around her, making her appear like the angel he knew she wasn't.

He glanced away. So what if Finley and he were at the same event? He wasn't the same heartsick youth she knew and, judging by the brittle way she held herself as the photographer posed the groom's attendants, she had changed, too. He could manage a few hours in her company. He was an adult. One with a full life that was about to become more complicated—and public.

In fact, the wedding might be doing him a favor. Once Screenweb announced the reality series based on EverAftr and his involvement in the first season, the media would dig into his romantic past. Finley might have resurfaced at a much more inopportune time and place. This way, he could rip the bandage off in relative privacy.

Assuming, that is, if he and Finley ever spoke. Judging by the way she glanced in every direction but his, it appeared she was as eager to reunite as he was. Made sense. She was the one who made it clear that summer was just a fling, and barely an entertaining one at that.

Damn his nearly perfect memory. Because now he recalled how her words landed, tearing fresh wounds with every precise syllable.

"So, what do you say? Food?" Lauren tugged at his hand.

He shook off the specters of the past and smiled at his sister. "Sure. Let's grab some crab puffs. Or whatever they're handing out."

He couldn't resist one last glimpse of Finley. She stood deep in conversation with another woman. If she felt his gaze on her, she didn't give any indication. He straightened his shoulders and pushed away from the corner, following Lauren as she wove her way through the merry throng of guests and toward the open bar.

Finley was ancient history. And she would stay that way.

But throughout the cocktail reception, the dinner and the dancing that followed, his memories would not remain submerged.

Finley thanked her dance partner—one of Grayson's colleagues from his venture capital firm—and left the bright lights and loud music of the dance floor. She passed various knots of guests deep in conversation, acknowledging those who nodded at her with a smile and a wave, and found an empty section of the terrace wreathed in shadows thanks to tall potted trees. She leaned on the stone balustrade and peered into the moonlit darkness of the vineyards below and the hills beyond, taking a moment to catch her breath.

And to still her pulse, which had raced all evening but not from dancing.

It took every ounce of self-control she had—and Finley had a deep, almost bottomless reserve of control, ask anyone—not to follow Will Taylor around with her gaze like the lovestruck girl she used to be. Not to leap on the stage and grab the microphone out of the lead singer's hand and demand an explanation from him. Not only, "Why are you here?" but "Why?" full stop. Why did he walk away, never to contact her again? Why did he let her go?

Why didn't he see past her words and realize she'd been forced to break up with him? If they were soul mates as he'd insisted, shouldn't he have seen the truth?

But then, soul mates weren't real. And the concept

of true love was a marketing tool used to sell greeting cards and animated films.

She sighed. She never was one to cry over spilled milk and Will was a grocery warehouse full of knocked over dairy products. A fifteen-year-old spill, so that milk was truly spoiled and lost. She would not give him the satisfaction of acknowledging his presence, even though she physically ached from the fierce battle going on between her head and her heart.

Her head said to ignore him. This was Grayson and Nelle's day. She had plenty of details and duties that required her attention. Will Taylor was not one of them.

Her heart wanted…oh, so many things. Too many to sort through. And this was exhibit B in why she hated weddings: they made people want to be with a special person who was meant for them and them alone. To believe such a person might actually exist. But then the next morning would arrive, bringing with it the inevitable champagne hangover and a cold dose of reality.

An alarm chimed and she took her phone out of her skirt pocket. One hour until Grayson and Nelle would get into the vintage Rolls-Royce with "Just Married" scrawled on the windows. Then the wedding would be at an end and she, too, could depart. The winery staff had assured her they would take care of getting the remaining guests safely to their next destination and cleaning up, leaving her free.

But free for what? The only employer she'd ever had was behind bars in a federal penitentiary. And since she'd helped to put him there, it was probably safe to say she wouldn't receive a sterling reference from him. Planning the wedding had kept her thoughts busy and her feet moving for the last year or so, but that had obviously come to a conclusion.

The wind ruffled the ends of her hair, the chill air cutting through the lace and satin of her gown. With no patio heater nearby, she was reminded it was indeed February. She put the phone away, intending to return to the dance floor, when she overhead a woman mentioning Grayson's name.

Finley peered around the potted tree. A few feet away, a couple stood in close embrace, no doubt thinking they had this corner to themselves. Not wanting to disturb them—or face questions about why she was skulking alone—she remained still.

The man laughed. "Sure, Grayson is a great guy. Really happy for him, especially after what happened."

"I noticed the ex-congressman didn't make an appearance," the original female speaker said, an arch note in her tone.

"Might have been difficult for him, considering he's in prison." The man laughed. "Regardless, don't think much love is lost there," he continued. "Can you imagine if you were Grayson and your father was found guilty of misappropriating campaign funds? Good thing Grayson's reputation was already solid in the venture capital community or he'd never be trusted with investors' money again."

Finley clenched her fists but stayed silent. The situation with Barrett was scandalous and sordid, but also sad. Grayson grew up hero-worshipping his father only to discover Barrett's feet were not only clay, but hollow and full of rot.

She would never forgive Barrett for what he did to his son.

"Grayson will be fine, but I do have to question his judgment," the woman said. "I mean, really, including his sister in the wedding? When she worked arm-in-arm with their father and must have been up to her neck in the same corruption? Wonder what strings were pulled to keep her out of prison."

Something hurt. Finley glanced down and realized her nails were digging into her palms.

The man laughed. "There's one set of rules for people like the Monk family and another for the rest of us. I'm surprised the dad was caught in the first place. C'mon, let's go say goodbye and get back to the hotel."

Finley counted to thirty and then peered around the tree again. The couple was gone. She shivered, and the goose bumps on her skin had nothing to do with the night breeze.

It was one thing to intellectually understand her career was gone, and any avenues she'd wish to take to return to politics were closed. It was another to have random people confirm she would be viewed with suspicion wherever she went. Even at her brother's wedding.

But at least the couple's derision wasn't pity. She was tired—so tired!—of soft voices asking if she was okay. Tired of whispered conversations and solicitous gazes behind her back, when acquaintances thought she couldn't see or hear them.

She always saw and heard them.

She rolled her eyes. Maybe cloying, maudlin expressions of condolence made other people feel better, but as the object of their sympathy, they turned her stomach. She should find the unknown couple and thank them for their honesty.

But at the moment, her new sister-in-law was due to change out of her wedding gown and into clothes more comfortable for travel. Finley had volunteered to ensure Nelle's dress made it to the specialty cleaners while Grayson and Nelle were on their honeymoon. She might as well check in to see if Nelle needed anything else.

Stepping out of the safety of the shadows, Finley walked briskly toward the large oak door leading to the winery's gift shop and, beyond it, the private rooms set aside for the event. She kept her gaze locked on her phone. Hopefully, anyone who spotted her would assume she was attending to important wedding-related duties and would think twice before intercepting her. She had her right hand stretched out to pull the door open, her head still down—

The heavy door swung out, almost hitting her. She stumbled backward. The stiletto heel of her left shoe caught, slid on a loose pebble. The shoe went in one direction, her foot in another. Her ankle twisted as her balance escaped her.

Stars of pain exploded, filling her vision. Her arms

flew out, flailing, her hands seeking something, anything to grasp. Her eyes slammed shut, anticipating the imminent rough landing on hard stone.

"I have you."

Solid, strong arms surrounded her. Her fingers clutched at fine wool covering firm biceps underneath as she scrambled to regain her footing. But when her left foot touched the ground, pain shot through her ankle, taking her breath away. She remained in the embrace of her Good Samaritan until the throbbing dulled enough for her other senses to register again, bringing her heartbeat and breathing back to something resembling normal. Warm hands continued to hold her, reassuring her she wouldn't fall.

After what felt like an eternity but was probably only a few seconds, Finley regained her balance enough to stand, keeping her weight on her good foot. The sting receded as she wriggled her bare toes. He ankle was just twisted, not sprained or broken. She exhaled and straightened up, and then turned to thank the person who came to her assist.

Her breath disappeared again.

Will.

Three

Will saw the accident happen as if in slow motion. The door began to swing out. The man pushing it open, his head turned, looking at his companion instead of checking to see if someone was on the other side. Finley, nose-deep in her phone as she headed for a direct collision. Her wide-eyed surprise as she narrowly avoided being hit by the solid oak doors. Her foot slipping, turning. Her scared gasp as she started to fall.

Will couldn't think. He refused to feel. He could only react. His pulse beat in his ears, a heavy percussion felt more than heard.

He caught her.

Finley's chest rose and fell in quick successive breaths and hyperventilation was added to his concerns until she got her breathing under control. He wrenched his gaze away, suddenly aware the lace of her gown did not fully conceal the swells of her breasts, teasing the shadowy valley between them.

"Are you okay?" he asked, his voice a rasp.

She nodded, her eyes remaining unfocused. Using his arm for leverage, she stood up straight. A wing of black hair fell across her face and she brushed it back with her free hand before turning to him. "Thank y—"

Her smile of gratitude froze. Shutters slammed down, rendering her gaze opaque. She dropped his arm as if she had just spotted a radioactive warning.

Over the last decade or so, he'd thought many times about what he would say if he bumped into her. Something smooth. Suave. Charming, but distant. A polite acknowledgment that would firmly indicate he had long since moved on and she was a nothing but a pleasant if fading memory.

"You should see a doctor about your ankle," he said, his voice raspy in his ears.

That was not one of the phrases he'd stored up all these years. His mind raced, seeking and discarding what to say next. Perhaps, "Hello, Finley, nice to see you?" But it wasn't nice. *Nice* was a word used to describe running into an old neighbor at the grocery store. *Nice* didn't cause throats to tighten and hands to sweat. *Nice* didn't bring images buried long ago to roaring life, sharper than ever.

She shook her head, tiny movements, but he saw them. Then she bent down and straightened the abandoned shoe on the terrace before slipping her left foot back into it. When she finally caught his eye, she smiled.

If smiles could freeze, he would be an ice sculpture. "Thank you for your advice," she said. "But what I need isn't your concern."

And never was, nor ever would be, her Arctic-chilled tone implied. "Of course I'm concerned. Anyone with common human decency would be. Maybe if you had some—" He bit the rest of his words back.

"If I had some…what? Decency?" If he thought the atmosphere was cold before, now it resembled an eternal winter. "You—" She snapped her crimson-dark lips closed as Lauren joined them.

"Hi." His sister gave Finley a friendly wave before tucking her left hand through his elbow and turning to him. "Sorry if I'm interrupting, but the band is playing my favorite song. You owe me a dance."

Finley's gaze zeroed in on Lauren's engagement and wedding rings, the solitaire diamond's size and brilliance evident even in the dim glow of the overhead string of lights. Her smile returned, wider and more brittle than before. "Excellent idea. You two go dance."

"Finley, this is Lauren. My—"

Finley held up her right hand, stopping his words. "Thank you for your assistance. Please, enjoy the rest of your evening." She nodded at Lauren and her smile faltered, only to appear again, smaller, but more genuine. "Both of you. Have fun. Now if you'll excuse me, I have bridal party duties that require my attention."

She turned, still a bit unsteady on her left foot, and yanked open the door to the winery's gift shop. "Get that ankle looked at," he called after her.

She gave no indication she heard him. The door slammed shut behind her.

Lauren crossed her arms over her chest. "What was that about?"

He shrugged, hoping his sister would interpret the movement as nonchalance and not because he was finding it difficult to form words, much less parse the emotions roiling through him. "She almost fell. I caught her."

Lauren's gaze narrowed. He cut her off before she could ask another pointed question. "You didn't tell me the groom was Barrett Monk's son."

Finley never talked about a brother. On the other hand, he was pretty sure he never mentioned Lauren or his other sister.

They'd had to sneak away from their respective duties to be together as it was. They hadn't spent a lot of their stolen time discussing family members.

"Why did I need to tell you?" Lauren looked at him as if he'd grown a third ear on his forehead. "The story was all over the national news. I've been to your place. You don't live under a rock."

Will shook his head. "Never mind." If he pursued this line of conversation, Lauren might ask him questions he wasn't in the mood to answer.

He never told his family about that summer. Lauren had been in high school and involved in her own teenage dramas at the time. And at first, he could hardly believe someone like Finley was his and so he didn't want to jinx it by telling too many people. Later, he realized that the relationship had been a mistake from the start and there was no reason to tell anyone the joke had been on him. "You said something about dancing?"

"Song's almost over now, but I'll accept another glass of wine."

"Deal. Lead on to the bar."

But as he followed Lauren through the crowd, the scent of pomegranate and spice—Finley's scent, warm and opulent and uniquely hers—remained with him, unlocking more memories he thought long lost. The sooner he left the wedding—the sooner he left California—the sooner he could put his past behind him and concentrate on his future.

It was going to be a long night.

Finley paused outside the room set aside for Nelle's use, taking a moment to smooth her hair, straighten her skirt and get her heartbeat under control. Her cheeks felt cool to the touch so hopefully her complexion was back to normal. There was nothing she could do about her vision, which still swam with the sight of the ginormous diamond ring and platinum wedding band on the hand of Will's companion.

She knocked on the door and waited for Nelle's cheerful "Come in!" before entering and taking the nearest chair, tucking her still-throbbing left ankle behind her right.

Nelle sat at the vanity table occupying the far wall.

Her hair was no longer in the complicated updo she wore for the wedding and she was brushing out the last of the curls. She'd already changed into gray trousers and a soft navy sweater Finley had seen her wear many times before—probably because the top had been a gift from Grayson.

Nelle caught Finley's gaze in the mirror and smiled. "Hi. You're early."

Finley glanced at Nelle's wedding gown, carefully draped over the sofa next to the vanity. "Looks like I'm late. Did you have any trouble getting out of the dress?"

Nelle shook her head and then swiveled so she faced Finley. "Yoselin helped. You just missed her," she said, referring to her matron of honor. "And your timing is perfect. I wanted a few minutes alone with you."

Finley lifted her eyes toward the ceiling. "I expected sentimental drivel from Grayson. But you, Nelle? I'm crushed."

"Even fairy godmothers get to be thanked."

Finley laughed. "I'm hardly a fairy godmother. If I could wave a wand and make problems disappear, I'd start with my own."

And she knew exactly what she would zap first. That portion of her mind that stubbornly retained memories of Will, despite her best efforts to delete them.

Her fingers still carried Will's impression. The smooth, fine wool of his jacket. The unbelievably broad shoulders. The hard, bunched muscles of his arms as he held her. The–

Too late, she realized Nelle was speaking.

"—doubt anyone with a magic wand could have planned a more wonderful day for Grayson and me. Honestly, no matter what words I use to thank you, they're inadequate." Nelle's eyes shimmered, causing Finley to glance down.

One of the things she appreciated the most about her new sister-in-law was Nelle's ability to remain calm when situations became fraught—at least in Finley's presence. A Nelle capable of impersonating a watering can was new to Finley, and while she supposed allowances must be made for brides on their wedding day, she wasn't up to dealing with other people's emotions. Not after Will Taylor. Not when Finley struggled to keep such a tight control on her own emotions, she wanted to scream from the exertion.

Her gaze landed on the pinprick spot of blood on her cream lace bodice, now a brown fleck. Little did Nelle know how flawed the day had turned out to be, at least for Finley. She straightened in her chair and looked Nelle in the eye. "Don't you dare cry. I sent the makeup artist home, and you still have photos to take in the getaway car."

Nelle laughed, and sniffed, and carefully dabbed the area under her eyes. "I wouldn't dream of it."

"Good." Finley nodded. "Because I rented a classic Rolls-Royce, and mascara stains are hell to get out of vintage leather."

"Speaking of getaway…" Nelle rose from the vanity and came to stand in front of Finley. She had a white letter-size envelope in her hand. "This is for you."

Finley's stomach squeezed, and for once that day Will had nothing to do with it. "I don't—I was happy to plan the wedding. In fact you did me a favor by letting me do it. But I don't need Grayson's or your money—I'll be fine—"

"Never in doubt." Nelle dropped into the chair next to her. "You're Finley Smythe."

Her stomach still roiled. But she managed her trademark smirk. "Damn straight I am."

"But—" Nelle held up the envelope "—even you can use a getaway. And I'm not referring to a car with 'Just Married' written on the windows."

Finley eyed the envelope and moved to stand, the better to grab the wedding gown and make a fast exit, but she sat back down when her ankle protested. "My transportation is already taken care of for tonight, thanks." She took her phone out and looked at the screen. "And speaking of getaways, it's almost time for you and Grayson to make yours. Are you all set? Do you have everything?" She opened the text app and started a new message to the winery staff while she continued her conversation with Nelle. "Let me check in and make sure the chef packed a to-go box for you and Grayson. Neither of you had enough to eat—"

Nelle laid her hand on top of Finley's, stopping her movements. Finley gave Nelle her best imperious stare, but Nelle's hand did not move. "What?" Finley asked.

"The wedding, the—" Nelle waved her free hand "—events of the last year. Despite everything, you constantly put Grayson and me first."

Finley narrowed her gaze and opened her mouth to protest.

Nelle cut her off with a firm shake of her head. "I've learned there is indeed a human being underneath that shark suit of yours, so don't give me your barracuda stare of death."

"Barracudas are fish, not sharks. And obviously my stare is not working, or you wouldn't have my hand still trapped."

"Sorry." Nelle sounded anything but apologetic. However, she released Finley's fingers. "You're always looking for ways to take care of us. And we appreciate it, more than we can express. But who takes care of you?"

Nelle's soft words reverberated in the silence that followed. Finley sat back in her chair, pinned by the force of her sister-in-law's gaze. Damn her ankle. Otherwise, she would already be far away. Away from Nelle's questions, away from ghosts of the past who materialized all too solidly, away from reminders that her carefully chosen life stratagems resulted in ruin. "I don't need anyone to take care of me. Obviously."

Nelle shook her head. "I didn't say anything about need. Of course you are more than capable of taking care of yourself. Let me try a different question—what are you going to do now that the wedding is over?"

"Go to the hotel, draw a hot bath and enjoy a fine bottle of wine." She checked her phone again. The basket of food for the newlyweds was already in the car. Another item she could check off her list. "And as soon as you and Grayson take off, I can put my plan in motion. Ready to go?"

Nelle remained seated. "And after the bath water is cold and the wine is gone? What are you doing next week? Next month? Next year? What are your goals, now that your past career has been cut off?"

Ouch. Finley regarded her sister-in-law. "I see I've taught you well since we met. Going for the jugular. Nice."

Nelle grinned at her. "I learned from the best." She waved the envelope. "I meant what I said earlier. Words cannot express how grateful we are to you. But maybe this gift will."

Finley finally took it from her. "I swear, if this is money—" She ripped the envelope open.

It didn't contain cash or a check. Instead, she pulled out sheets of paper. What looked like a map and printouts of instructions and security codes and directions to...

She caught Nelle's gaze. Her sister-in-law was beaming.

Finley raised her eyebrows. "You're giving me your honeymoon? I mean, I love my brother—and you—but don't you think three's a crowd?"

"One of our honeymoons," corrected Nelle. "Grayson surprised me a few days ago with his wedding gift. We're going to Masaai Mara in Kenya. Which leaves this—" she picked up a sheet of paper that had fallen from Finley's lap and returned it to her "—open and available. And we both thought you should take our place."

The words blurred on the pages. "But—"

"No *buts*. It's all arranged. Two weeks of luxurious pampering with no one else around and nothing to do but enjoy yourself. And you can invite a friend to join you."

Finley ignored the last part. The only people she would consider bringing with her on a lavish vacation were going on their honeymoon in Africa. Not that she was vacationing in the first place. "This is very kind of you both, but I can't—"

"Can't what?" Nelle stared down Finley. "Can't miss work? Turns out that isn't a problem."

"I taught you too well," Finley muttered. "Harsh, but true."

"I'm sorry." This time the apology was sincere. "But Fin, please, we want to do something for you. And we thought you might appreciate an opportunity to decompress and reassess. The media attention and public scrutiny have been overwhelming for Grayson and me at times. We can only imagine how much harder this past year has been for you."

Because everyone thinks you were party to Barrett's corruption as his campaign manager and chief of staff.

Nelle didn't have to say the words. Finley heard them loud and clear. Derision from strangers she could handle. Pity from acquaintances was uncomfortable and distasteful, but she could brush it off. Nelle and Grayson feeling sorry for her… That was overwhelming. And not in a good way.

"I can't accept this." Finley stood, putting all her weight on her uninjured foot. "I appreciate the thought. But I don't need to decompress." She handed the papers back to Nelle.

Nelle rose and placed the printouts on her abandoned chair. "Even sharks need rest."

"That's what the hot bath and bottle of wine are for." Finley managed to make it to the sofa and picked up the wedding gown without too much of a limp. "I'm going to put the dress somewhere safe, and then I'll meet you at the car."

"If you change your mind—"

"I won't."

"If you do," Nelle continued, unfazed, "all the information should also be in your email inbox."

"See you in fifteen minutes." Finley exited the room, the gown in her possession. The need to protect the delicate fabric that overfilled her arms provided a convenient excuse for walking gingerly.

Finley lived by three rules: Never let others see her at anything but her best. Never react when someone scored a direct hit on one of her weaker spots. Never look back, only forward.

She'd broken all of them in the last five hours.

She *hated* weddings.

Four

Finley did not get her hot bath or her bottle of wine. Last-minute questions from the staff kept her at the winery long after the guests had left. By the time she reached her suite at the nearby hotel, she had just enough energy to put ice on her ankle—hours too late, but still—and fall into bed.

Sunlight streaming through the windows she forgot to cover woke her before she could get her much-needed eight hours of sleep. She blinked and sat up, at first too bleary to remember where she was. Then the memories of the night before flooded back, and she fell against the pillows.

Not every memory was bad. She'd never seen her brother look so happy. Joyous didn't even begin to describe his expression when he looked at Nelle. And

Nelle's gaze overflowed with love and delight. The two of them were almost enough to make Finley reconsider her stance on whether *happily-ever-after* existed outside of nonsensical fairy tales.

Almost.

Because along with her memories of Grayson and Nelle driving away in wedded bliss came the feel of Will's arms around her: warm, sturdy, solid as steel. His unforgettable scent, woodsy and multilayered. The scorn in his voice when he assured her his offer of assistance was only out of common human decency, implying she lacked the same.

Will's companion, her proprietary left hand on his arm bearing an unmissable set of wedding rings.

Finley flung the covers off. She needed to get up and start her day. Start her life, for that matter. Nelle was right about one thing last night. Finley had thrown herself into planning the ceremony and the reception that followed. And while she excelled at the task, she recognized she also used it as a distraction. As long as she was neck-deep in seating charts and catering negotiations and band contracts, she could ignore thinking long term.

Until this morning.

She picked up the phone from the bedside table and ordered room service for breakfast. Then she grabbed her toiletries and headed to the bathroom to take a bracing shower while waiting for her food to arrive. Since people liked to compare her to a shark, she might as well act like one and swim forward, never backward.

The morning sun blazed bright, although rain was forecast for the West Coast later that afternoon. Television meteorologists were making worried noises about "the storm of the century." But Finley had grown up in California and she was well aware most weather events were given hyperbolic names simply because anything that deviated from the sunny norm was unusual—and the grandiose titles made for good TV ratings. She dressed to spite the predicted precipitation in a long, diaphanous skirt and a thin silk sweater with a low V-neck. And when room service knocked on her door, she directed the server to wheel the cart to the terrace, the better to enjoy the warm rays.

The eggs were done to perfection, the orange juice was fresh-squeezed and the bacon had just enough crunch. Her mood lifted with every bite. So what if Barrett was in a federal penitentiary and her name was mud? Mud was merely soil and water. It could be wiped clean. She was good at her job and had invaluable experience navigating the halls of power in Washington, DC. Besides, Barrett's scandal had long faded from the evening news and the late night comedy shows, his story replaced by others' misdeeds and follies. She started to make a list of people to call to arrange coffee or drinks—

Her phone rang. She frowned. Grayson and Nelle should be enjoying first class in the sky, on their way to London for a few days before making the connection to Nairobi, and she couldn't think of who else would need to get a hold of her so early in the day. A glance at the screen revealed her caller was Sadiya Khan, and Finley's frown deepened. She answered. "Please tell me you're calling to gossip about the wedding."

"Did you know Barrett was involved with Senator O'Donnell's wife? Or rather, soon-to-be former wife?" Finley's lawyer asked without preamble.

"What? No." Suddenly, breakfast did not sit well in her stomach. Senator O'Donnell was embroiled in an insider trading scandal that made Barrett's campaign finance fraud look like a five-year-old raiding his piggy bank by comparison. "Why do I get the feeling there's a second part to your question?"

Sadiya sighed. "Erica O'Donnell wrote a book."

"People do that," Finley responded. "What does—"

"She's trying to create a bidding war among publishers. We got a heads-up tip that you're featured in the manuscript."

Finley sat back in her chair. "Why would I be in Erica O'Donnell's book? I think we've spoken maybe…twice?…in the last ten years."

"She claims you're the one who originally put together the insider trading ring and then you leaked her husband's involvement to the press."

"What?" Finley took the phone away from her ear, stared at it in disbelief, then returned it. "What the— that's utterly preposterous—why would I do that?"

Sadiya sighed. "According to her, you were angry Senator O'Donnell was the frontrunner for the presidential nomination and wanted to wreck his political career."

A cold, hard ball settled in Finley's stomach. She wasn't sure if it was born of rage or frustration or a combination of both. "This is ridiculous. Why would I care if O'Donnell got the nomination or not—"

"You wanted Barrett to be the nominee, so you could pull the strings behind the scenes. But Barrett refused to challenge Senator O'Donnell because he didn't want Erica to be hurt if their affair was exposed. So he instead announced his early retirement from Congress—"

"Wait, what?" Finley blinked several times, hoping the movement would help her process what she was hearing. "Barrett stepped down because of his health."

"Not according to Erica. He was chivalrously protecting her reputation. In retaliation, you went on a scorched earth campaign and blew the whistle on Barrett's fraud, while setting up the O'Donnells for insider trading. She goes into explicit detail—"

The ball in Finley's stomach was definitely rage. The world turned hazy white with edges tinged with red. "That's the most awful, outrageous, scurrilous—"

"We're going to fix this." Sadiya's calm tone cut through the fog enveloping Finley. "She's making even more extreme claims about other people."

"More extreme?" Something vibrated against Finley's ear and she realized it was her phone, due to her trembling hand. "Hard to believe that's possible."

"She's flinging dirt in all directions to see what will stick."

"And she knows it will stick to me, thanks to Barrett's scandal." Finley's nose burned and there was a suspicious prickling in the corner of her eyes. She swallowed and forced the tears back. She would not give Erica O'Donnell the satisfaction of making her cry, even if out of rage, even if no one saw her do so.

"What Erica knows is she's up to her neck in the same schemes as her husband and also facing indictment and serious jail time. She's creating diversions, hoping to send the investigators and the press off on wild-goose chases."

"You know how the media works," Finley said through numb lips. "Write headlines first, retract only if forced to later."

"Not all. But some outlets, yes," Sadiya agreed.

Normally, Finley appreciated Sadiya's no-nonsense, cut-through-the-bullshit approach. But at times, like now, she'd appreciate a little fudging of the truth, just for reassurance. A large, albeit invisible, weight pressed down on her shoulders. "Am I to assume a tsunami of reporters is headed my way? Again?"

Sadiya was silent for a moment. "I'm speaking to the best defamation lawyers in the country. We'll get you cleared. But for now…"

Finley screwed her eyes shut. She definitely regretted the orange juice. The citric acid burned holes in her stomach. "But for now, brace for impact."

"That's my advice."

"Okay." Finley took a deep breath, thankful Grayson and Nelle were headed overseas and would be difficult to reach for the next month. They should enjoy their honeymoon without having to wade through yet more scandal thrown at their family.

As for her, she would get through this. She got through the press circus when Grayson abruptly dropped out of his run for Congress. She survived the round of constant media badgering when Barrett was indicted for fraud, and the second, even more ferocious round when he went on trial. This was merely Erica O'Donnell trying to drum up interest in what was no doubt a sensational piece of fiction, hastily written to make money before she, too, went to federal prison.

"We'll put the brakes on as fast as we can," Sadiya said. "In the meantime—"

"Don't knock over any banks and draw even more attention. Got it." She opened her eyes and glanced across the lush garden courtyard that separated her cottage suite from the others. The morning continued to be gorgeous. More people were taking advantage of the momentary sunshine and temperate breezes to also have their breakfast on their private terraces. Lucky people, who probably had no concern deeper than getting in a round of golf or touring nearby wineries. People like—

Will.

She froze. No, she did not conjure up his image. That was Will on the terrace directly opposite hers, separated only by a strip of emerald green lawn lined with profusely flowering rosebushes.

If she thought Will looked more attractive than any

human had a right to in his suit the night before, that was nothing to seeing Will in a T-shirt that clung to his broad shoulders and skimmed over what appeared to be an impressive set of pecs. Those were new, her brain couldn't help noticing. Well-worn jeans draped just so over narrow hips and powerful thighs. He was carrying two cups of coffee and thankfully wasn't looking in her direction—because he was talking to his female companion from the night before, who laughed and affectionately punched his shoulder before taking one of the cups from him.

"Finley? Did I lose you?"

"I'm here." Finley almost knocked over her chair in her haste to get inside her suite and draw the curtains across the windows before Will could spot her staring at him with her mouth half-open like a drooling teenager at her first pop idol concert.

Not that she cared if Will saw her, obviously all alone and frowning into her phone. Not at all.

No, she only went inside because she'd learned it was better not to give the press anything when they were on the hunt. And for all she knew, journalists were already descending upon the hotel. Grayson and Nelle's wedding hadn't exactly been a secret—anyone with a gift for research on the internet would be able to find the details—and if they weren't already prowling the grounds, they would be soon.

"Sorry," she continued, locking the French doors behind her. She tucked the phone between her right shoulder and ear and then opened her suitcase on the luggage rack, not caring to fold her clothes before throwing them in. "I decided to multitask and pack while we talked."

"Good idea. I don't know who else was tipped off about the book. And regardless, it will become public knowledge sooner than later." Finley heard her slight intake of breath, which she knew meant Sadiya was considering her words. "Do you want me to call our security contractors? I can have guards at your place in a few hours."

Finley stopped taking clothes off hangers and sank onto the bed. "You think I need a security detail? Seriously?"

"Senator O'Donnell is popular with a certain segment that likes to make threats on dark corners of social media. It's only a precaution," Sadiya hastened to add. "You haven't received any that I know of. Just thinking ahead."

"Hold on a minute." No, she did not want guards. The last thing she wanted was to become a virtual prisoner in her place of residence, mostly because she was currently residing in the guest cottage on Barrett's estate, a three-hour drive southeast from the Bay Area. Barrett had been in ill health even before his indictment, and Finley had moved in to oversee his medical care. She'd sublet her Washington, DC, apartment, and she never had looked for a new home of her own.

Too many memories. Too many people angry at her. Finley knew she'd done the right thing by alerting the authorities to Barrett's fraud, but others saw her as disloyal. A turncoat. A traitor to the man who married her mother and took her in when she was a three-month old baby, and to the Monk family name, which had been prominent in California politics for generations. According to them, she was the viper in the family's breast who brought down a dynasty and destroyed not only her stepfather, but her brother's promising political career. It didn't matter to them that Grayson chose of his own free will to drop out of his race for Congress.

She took the phone away from her ear and opened her email app. She started scrolling—yes. Nelle had made good on her promise and Finley had all the information she needed. Nelle even promised appropriate clothes would be waiting for her since, as Nelle phrased it, "your usual wardrobe might not be appropriate."

Finley put the phone back up to her ear. "I have a better idea."

Will watched Finley stalk into her suite and close the door behind her, most of her breakfast left untouched on the table. He hoped he wasn't the reason why she felt the need to abandon her food, then mentally shook his head at his own ego. He didn't mean a thing to Finley Smythe, except perhaps as a lingering bad odor from somewhere vaguely in her past.

At least she appeared steady on her ankle, not that he paid much attention to that part of her anatomy. When he blinked, the image of Finley's curved hips and long legs, revealed by the morning sunlight streaming through her thin skirt, was seared on the inside of his eyelids.

"Ground control to Major Will." Lauren waved her hand in his face. "Can you hear me?"

"Sorry." He'd spent enough time dwelling on Finley. Still, his gaze would not leave the spot where he last saw her. "You were saying?"

"I've been thinking about the television series. Are you *sure* you want to do it?"

That got his attention. "Why?"

"It's just…" Lauren chewed on the inside of her cheek, a nervous habit she'd had since childhood. "A TV show… It seems so…public."

"Of course it's public. It's marketing."

"Yeah, but the show is about *you*."

"Not just me."

"So you could drop out of appearing and production would still go forward?"

Will sipped his coffee, considering his words. "Screenweb bought the series based on my participation in the first season. Without me, they said it was just another reality dating series and they weren't interested. If I don't appear on camera, then no, they won't move forward. But the goal is to hook viewers and run for many years," he added.

"Which the series won't do if *you* don't successfully find someone," Lauren pointed out. "The whole world will be focused on you. If you don't end up marrying whoever the app matches you with, it's bad news not only for the series but for EverAftr as a company. Tell me you've thought this through."

He'd spent most of the sleepless night before doing nothing but thinking it through. "Our algorithm matches people based not only on their likes and dislikes, but also on intangible strengths and weaknesses as well as communication styles. It's why our customers have had such success. There's no reason why people won't be successful on camera as well." He smiled. "Are you doubting my work?"

Lauren rolled her eyes. "Of course not." She held up her left hand, her rings sparkling in the morning light. "Reid and I are proof your work is brilliant. But this isn't meeting someone privately via the app. It's a risk."

"You know the questionnaires and tests are extensive and highly vetted. I've made my preferences very clear." He'd double-checked them after seeing Finley again. He'd emphasized constancy, steadiness and dependability in his answers—all things that Finley had proved not to possess.

"If you say so." Lauren did not sound convinced.

He smiled. "It seems you don't believe the answers we've prepared for the press. Here's one more reason. Ji-Hoon is one of the producers."

Lauren's mouth formed an O. A former neighbor of their parents, Ji-Hoon Park had been one of Will's earliest cheerleaders. He helped Will get his first job in tech, and later introduced Will to people who became his future business partners. When Will started exploring the idea that turned into EverAftr, Ji-Hoon gave him the seed capital. "How's he doing? I haven't spoken to him lately. I need to call him."

"The last round of chemotherapy was tough, but he's hanging in. And he's thrilled to return to the industry, as he calls it." Ji-Hoon had tried to break into film and television acting as a young man, but roles for Asian men had been few and hard to come by. He returned to Illinois and eventually became a successful commercial real estate broker, but never lost his dream of making a splash in show business. Now Will had the opportunity to return all the favors Ji-Hoon did him by bringing Ji-Hoon on board as a producer on the series.

"And," Will continued, "we put a condition on the sale of the series to Screenweb. They'll team up with shelters and nonprofits working to prevent partner abuse and run an awareness campaign before every episode. EverAftr is earmarking fifteen percent of our revenue for those organizations."

"You could have led with that." Lauren flopped into the nearest chair and took out her phone, indicating she was through arguing with him.

"Now you know." He saluted Lauren with his mug, and then put it down on the low table next to her. "I have a long drive to Los Angeles. I should return to my room to pack. Thanks for the coffee."

She looked up. "Take the inland route. It's not as pretty as the coast, but faster."

"I live in Chicago where February equals dark and cold. I'm not going to miss my chance to catch ocean views."

"Forecasters are predicting a major storm," Lauren warned. "I'm glad my flight is leaving before the rain is supposed to hit."

"You forget I worked in Santa Monica for a few years. I laugh at California's attempts at weather."

She shook her head. "Just drive safely."

He kissed the top of her head. "I should be back in time to say goodbye before you leave for the airport. But if by some chance I miss you, have fun in Tokyo. Say hi to Reid."

He chuckled as he left. Chicago's rain was freezing in February. And if wasn't rain, it was sleet. And if it wasn't sleet, it was a snowstorm. A little California precipitation? Child's play.

Hours later, his knuckles white on his car's steering wheel as he tried to peer out the windshield, the wipers moving at high speed helpless against the torrential rain, he was no longer laughing.

Five

Finley attempted to push her hair out of her eyes, but the wet strands stayed plastered to her skin. Of all the days for weather forecasters to be right, they had to pick this one. She shivered. The skirt and sweater she'd thrown on that morning were little protection against the chilled wind and stinging rain.

At least she found Running Coyote Ranch. And not a moment too soon. What should have been a relatively easy six-hour drive south from Napa to Santa Barbara had stretched into nine hours thanks to the weather. She'd wanted to arrive before sunset but now the sky was completely dark, the moon and stars extinguished by thick clouds. Almost blinded by the heavy rain, she'd inched her way up the narrow canyon road with only her car's headlights to guide her. After what felt like a decade since she exited the highway, she reached the top of the hill and pulled into a wide circular drive—and upon leaving the car, stepped into a puddle she'd swear was big enough to go kayaking in, ensuring her sandal-encased feet were as wet as the rest of her.

This was what she got for not packing an umbrella, not that it would have been any help. The wind would have blown it inside out within a matter of minutes. She pulled up Nelle's email on her phone and found the entry code to punch into the keypad next to the immense carved doors. "Please work, please work, please work," she chanted under her breath. She was in no mood to get back into the car and search for alternate accommodations in the small community at the bottom of the long, twisty road she just crawled up.

The keypad made a clicking noise. Finley tugged on the doorknob. The door pulled open with ease. She crossed the threshold—

Oh. Wow. Yes.

Yes, this would do nicely as a place to stay for a few weeks, until Sadiya and her colleagues could get a better handle on the response to Erica O'Donnell's explosive claims.

According to Nelle's email, Running Coyote Ranch was built in 1928 by a now-forgotten silent film star, who spared no expense to create a haven where she and her fellow celluloid legends could relax and play in private. Designed in the Spanish Colonial Revival style, a popular architectural choice in Southern California at the time, the ranch was a stunning example of what money could buy—especially when there was access to Hollywood craftsman, many of whom had made the two-hour journey north from the film studios in Los Angeles to construct the ranch's main house and outbuildings.

Finley left her suitcase to drip on the thick square terra-cotta tiles in the expansive entryway. She ventured into large living area just beyond, marveling at the colorful smaller tiles that outlined the stucco arched doorways and the intricately painted wood beams that held up the coffered ceiling. One wall was mostly fireplace, built out of roughhewn stone, tall enough for Grayson—who was well over six feet— to stand in. Chestnut brown leather sofas, wide and long enough to comfortably hold a spooning couple for a nap, faced each other in front of the wrought iron fire screen. Additional chairs, some draped with blankets that looked so soft they must be pure cashmere, were arranged to create areas for conversations. Bookcases lined the other three walls, filled with colorful book spines interspersed with displays of pottery and artistic photographs of Southern Californian landscapes, while deeply piled sheepskin rugs were scattered across the floor, adding additional notes of warmth and coziness. Beyond the arched doorway, she caught a glimpse of additional rooms, also decorated in the height of luxurious rustic chic.

She couldn't wait to explore. But—she took a step and her wet skirt wrapped around her legs, chilling her anew—first, she needed to change her clothes. And maybe get a good night's sleep.

She returned to the entryway to recover her bag and discovered a binder on the long, low bench set against the wall. An envelope with her name on it rested on top. She flipped through the binder first, noting it held a map of the ranch, a plan of the main house with her room's location marked on it, plus any instructions she would need for the house's appliances during her stay. Inside the envelope was a card from Grayson and Nelle.

Dearest Finley,
We knew you wouldn't be able to resist. Welcome to Running Coyote! Since this was originally meant to be our honeymoon, the staff already had instructions not to disturb guests until asked for. Mariam Stern, the chief of staff, will be expecting your phone call when you want housekeeping services. We planned to do our own cooking and the kitchen should be fully stocked, but the ranch has a chef on standby. If you'd like your meals prepared, you can arrange that with Mariam.

Finley nodded. That would be among her immediate priorities in the morning. Food should only exist already arranged on a plate or in a take-out container as far as she was concerned.

Mariam's husband, Tim, is the ranch manager. We told him you're an excellent equestrienne and he has horses ready for you if you want

to go riding. The Sterns live in the compound at
the bottom of the hill and cell phone service can
be spotty in the mountains, so there's a CB radio
in the kitchen in case of emergency.

Running Coyote has a heated Olympic-size
swimming pool and spa, a fully equipped gym,
and the hiking trails are spectacular. Oh, and
help yourself to anything in the bar as well.
Have a wonderful time! And we hope you
brought someone special with you...
Nelle and Grayson.

She rolled at her eyes at the last sentence. Like she'd
had any time over the last decade or so to nurture a relationship. Besides, she'd probably combust of frustrated
irritation if she were stuck on the ranch for days on end
with anyone but maybe Grayson or Nelle. And even
then, it would be a close race as to which one of them
would grow sick of the other's company the fastest. She
resolutely put the image of Will, laughing at something
his companion said, out of her mind. His companion,
who wore a spectacular set of wedding rings.

Finley folded the card and placed it back in the envelope, then tucked it and the binder under her arm as
she followed the directions to the guest suite. Her own
company was perfectly sufficient. Even if the ranch
screamed "romantic getaway" around every corner
and she was essentially on a honeymoon of one.

She opened the door to the suite and instantly con-
gratulated herself on accepting Nelle's offer. The
three connected rooms—a sitting room that led to a

bedroom and an adjoining bathroom—were the epit-
ome of hospitable luxury.

She couldn't wait to take a long, hot bath in the
deep tub, big enough to comfortably stretch out in.
And then there was the bed—in this case, a king-size
four-poster with the fluffiest white duvet she'd ever
seen, a rust-and-brown cashmere blanket at the foot,
and so many pillows even Finley, a notorious bedding hog who loved to tuck herself in with a mountain
of goose down around her, was satisfied. The closet
was open, allowing her to catch a glimpse of enough
long-sleeved plaid shirts, denim jackets, jeans and
cowboy boots to clothe the entire cast of a revival of
Oklahoma! And if Finley's first action was to grab
the bottle of white wine sitting on the table tucked
into the picture-perfect reading alcove, well, she was
officially unemployed and on vacation.

She didn't bother with the wineglasses placed next
to the bottle.

Will regretted not taking his sister's advice to take
the inland route between Napa and Los Angeles instead of the coastal highway. If he had, maybe he'd
already be at his destination instead of just creeping
by Santa Barbara, which was still one hundred miles
north of LA.

The rain was relentless. He slowed his speed even
farther and tried to keep a decent following distance
between himself and the vehicle in front of him, but
the poor visibility, especially now that night had
fallen, did not help. He blinked, his eyes scratchy and

dry from focusing so hard—and red taillights suddenly lit up in front of him, far too close for comfort.

He slammed on his brakes. The rear end of his rented Porsche Cayman fishtailed. He steered into the slide and brought the car under control, just in time to keep the Cayman's front bumper from sliding into the pickup truck directly in his path. By some miracle, the car following Will managed to avoid a collision as well.

Adrenaline still pumping hard through his veins, he peered through the windshield. The deluge let up just enough for him to see that the highway had been turned into a parking lot. Cars that had once been steadily, if slowly, flowing down the road were motionless.

He sighed and dug down deep to find his well of patience. He'd need it.

Forty minutes later, Will had progressed only two miles. Worse, the rhythmic sweep of the wipers and the syncopated patter of rain on the car's roof were inducing drowsiness. He tried loud music to stay awake. He tried blasting the air conditioner. But he finally gave in to an inescapable fact: he had to get off the road or he would fall asleep at the wheel. The car's navigation system indicated the next available exit was Lobos Canyon, but it lacked symbols for hotels or even a fast-food restaurant...

Wait. Lobos Canyon. He knew Lobos Canyon. Of course.

He left a quick phone message for Lauren and then took the off-ramp as soon as he got to it. The directions came back easily to him, even in the dark and rain, and before long he turned onto the steep road that wound up into the hills. He was so intent on not missing a curve and accidentally plunging off the side of the canyon that he missed the first driveway that led to his destination. The road was too narrow to turn around safely in the dark, and he didn't trust the Porsche's tires—designed to sail down smoothly paved freeways—on the muddy, stone-filled terrain. That left him the second driveway, meant for delivery vehicles, horse trailers and tractors. When he arrived at the end of the gravel road, he realized he was closer to the stable than he was to the main house. Fine, he would just have to walk the rest of the way. Across a field. A wet, sludge-filled field.

By the time Will reached the residence and punched the access code to unlock the rear service door, the parts of his clothes that weren't covered in a thick layer of mud were soaked through. Water dripped down the nape of his neck and off his nose while his sneakers squelched with every step, leaving dirty puddles in his wake. Not wanting to traipse dirt through the main living quarters, he located the nearby laundry facilities. He kicked off his shoes and left them to air out on the utilitarian tile. Then he stripped off his shirt, wrung it out as much as he could and put it on an adjacent rack to dry.

His jeans were molded to his skin. He would deal with getting out of them later. Preferably just before jumping into a hot shower.

His laptop remained in the Porsche, but his sodden suitcase presented another problem. Rather than risk trailing muddy water through the residence, he grabbed a change of clothes—luckily, the inside of his bag was still dry—and his dopp kit, leaving the rest of his things with his shoes and shirt. Then he set off to find accommodations for the night.

Reid and Lauren had told him on his last visit that they always kept the guest wing ready in case of unexpected drop-ins. And if anyone fit that description, it was him. The house was dark, but his gift for remembering even small details came to his rescue. He easily found the stairs that led to the private suite. The door noiselessly swung open, revealing the sitting room with two closed doors, one leading to the spacious bedroom and the other to a bathroom that would be at home in a five-star luxury hotel.

He could almost feel the warm spray of the shower on his skin now. He dropped his things on a nearby chair and opened the door to the bathroom, unbuttoning his jeans as he walked into the space—

And froze.

Several items hit his brain's processing center, all at once.

One, the bathroom was not dark, as he expected it to be, but lit by flickering candles perched on the shelves that lined the wall between the oversize clawfoot bathtub and the walk-in shower.

Two, the air was heavy with steam and smelled of roses.

Three, the bathtub was filled with foamy bubbles. And floating in the midst of the bubbles, her head leaned against the wall of the tub and her eyes closed, was a nude Finley.

Six

The bath water was steaming hot, the wine went down deliciously smooth and Finley was finally, for what felt like the first time in over a year, utterly at peace. Oh, sure, her life was still stuck in the same place and the specter of Erica O'Donnell's egregious claims hung over her, but at the moment? Pure bliss.

If this bathroom was any indication of the care and attention paid to every detail by the ranch's owners and staff, she was very much going to enjoy her stay. She had her pick of bubble baths and foaming bath powders. Candles came thoughtfully paired with a lighter, making it easy to set them ablaze and appreciate their flickering ambiance. There was a tray to place across the tub should she feel like reading while reveling in a soak—she'd noticed the sitting room attached to the bedroom came with fully loaded book-cases. And there were cleverly hidden speakers if she wanted to listen to music.

She chose a bubble bath with roses on the label, the scent transporting her to a time when all she had to care about during long summer days and the too-short nights was finding the most secluded spot in the garden in which to meet her love. But she was too tired to concentrate on words on a page and couldn't be bothered to find tunes to match her mood. The slight lapping of water at the tub's edges as she shifted was music enough to her ears.

All was calm, all was dimly lit and warm. She found herself drifting in and out of consciousness, never falling truly asleep but lulled into a waking dream.

A dream starring Will. A Will who broke into a wide smile whenever he spotted her. Who never hesitated to hug her, to caress her, to even pick her up and spin her around as if it were the most natural thing in the world. As if she were the type of person who should be touched once her consent was given, frequently and with care. As if she should be held.

Such ideas had been foreign to her before she met Will. Her mother must have picked her up as an infant, surely? But by the time Finley could start storing memories, Grayson had arrived. She became the "big girl," who shouldn't want or need to be carried like her baby brother.

Then her mother had fallen ill, and neither Finley nor Grayson were held much. Finley's recollections of her mother weren't numerous, and mostly revolved around a dim, quiet room when their mother was intermittently home from chasing miracle cures interspersed with hospital stays. Finley and Grayson would be ushered in to kiss their mother good-night, but recollections of other activities weren't forthcoming.

She couldn't remember any gestures of affection from Barrett. But Grayson's warm, open heart must have come from somewhere. Or maybe he was born with it.

For all that Barrett wasn't her biological father, she was the one who most resembled him when it came to personality. She used to pride herself on being as cutthroat as he was.

Until that summer. With Will. A summer that opened up new possibilities. New avenues. A whole new way of being. A new person for her to become.

What would have happened if she had refused to believe Barrett, told him firmly to stay out of her life? Chose Will and a vastly uncertain future? Who would she be now?

She opened her eyes.

Will stood before her, his eyes wide, his mouth moving but no sound coming out.

She closed her eyes again. Of course she saw Will. It was only natural her mind would conjure him, after running into him at the wedding. She was warm and relaxed and the wine burned low in her stomach. Who else would she think about but—

A shirtless Will, whose shoulders and chest had

not been that broad and developed when she knew him. And he definitely hadn't had six-pack abs. Or worn well-made jeans that clung to his narrow hips and powerful legs and...wait.

Her eyes flew open again. "What in the everlasting holy f—"

"Sorry—I had no idea you were here—" Will slapped his left hand over his eyes as his feet backpedaled, his other hand outstretched to fumble for the door. "This isn't—I just wanted to get off the freeway—"

"What the—why in the—how are you here?" Bubbles. The bubbles, which had once heaped high, were almost gone. She was barely covered. Will could see, well, everything.

Not that she was ashamed. Nudity was a natural human condition, and she had no issues disrobing in front of other adults at, say, the changing room at the gym. But he was *Will*. And she swore Will would never see her naked again.

Never.

And she would be damned if she acted like a demure virgin in front of him, using her hands and arms to cover the pertinent bits while wearing nothing but a blush. Been there, done that with him, and that ship had long sailed, anyway. She splashed around, her thoughts as frantic as her movements, until she finally remembered the plush towel on the low bench next to the tub. She reached for it. "How did you—did you break in? No, wait, how did you even know Running Coyote existed? Are you following me? What the *hell*, Will?"

She wrapped the towel around her while still sitting in the bathtub. The towel soaked up water and became heavy and sodden, but at least she could keep her vow to never be nude in front of him again.

Will continued to back up, his hip encountering the edge of the Carrara marble counter. He muttered but kept his hand in front of his face. "Sorry," he continued to repeat as he edged his way toward the doorway. "I'll give you your privacy—" He hit a sharp corner and grunted in pain. "Damn it."

Finley huffed. "Oh, for crying out loud, turn around and use your eyes before the bath turns ice cold and I die of hypothermia."

His outreached hand finally found the doorknob. "I'm leaving—"

"Now," she ordered.

"Be careful. The floor can be slipper—"

"I can exit a bathtub just fine, thank you very much."

"You hurt your ankle the other day. The stone tile is a hazard—"

She resisted the urge to throw the loofah at him. "Get. Out."

Will closed the door behind him. Finley exhaled, trying to get her breath under control. She was trembling, and she was pretty sure it had nothing to do with wearing a soaking wet towel while sitting in a tub of cooling water.

What is Will Taylor doing at Running Coyote?

* * *

Will leaned against the closed door to the bathroom. His mind, so good at running several computational problems simultaneously, was stuck in a loop and had no indication of escaping it.

Finley Smythe was here. At his brother-in-law's ranch getaway.

A nude Finley, luscious and glowing in the candlelight. Her sharply angled face relaxed, appearing younger than when they first met. Her breasts, perfectly sized for his hands, almost but not quite hidden, their deep-rose peaks breaking through the foam. The dark triangle between her legs, just visible beneath the water.

Only his shock kept him from making a bigger fool of himself in front of her. Because if he thought he was immune to Finley Smythe, the heavy fullness in his cock as he relived his first sight of her told a different story. Sometimes he couldn't decide if having a near photographic memory was a blessing or a curse.

But what was she doing here? He knew Reid and Lauren and the newly married Monks were friends—after all, that was why Will was able to attend the small, highly exclusive wedding. Apparently that friendship extended to Finley. Although, at the reception, Finley and Lauren didn't seem to be well acquainted.

He shook his head, hoping it would jog his thoughts free. It didn't matter who, when or why. The pertinent facts were easy enough to parse. Finley was here.

So was he. The weather was awful. Neither of them should be out in the storm.

The ranch had far more than one bathroom and bedrooms were plentiful. If he stayed the night, the house was big enough that he didn't have to set eyes on her again before he left in the morning.

So why was he still lingering outside this particular bathroom door? Damned if he knew. He grabbed his things from where he had flung them on the chair and strode to exit the guest suite.

A crash from the bathroom stopped him in his tracks. He turned back and was knocking on the door within seconds. "Finley?"

"Go. Away." The words were gritted, as if uttered from between her teeth. As if she were in pain.

"What happened? Do you need a doctor?"

"What is it with you and your rescuer complex? I'm fine. I knocked over a candle, that's—ow!"

Visions of flames surrounding Finley dashed through his head. "I'm coming in."

"I don't need your hel—" Her voice trailed into a loud yelp.

That did it. Will opened the door and flipped on the light switch. Finley sat on the wooden bench built into the wall next to the tub, wrapped in a soaking-wet towel. The remains of a large glass candleholder littered the floor. But it was the blood, on the tile and smeared over Finley's feet, that caused his stomach to flip. "What happened?"

"I stepped on broken glass and cut my foot," she grumbled. "And who said you could come in?"

"You did," he said. "By yelling in pain."

"I did no such thing."

"Someone did. And since the staff don't live in and I know this place isn't haunted, you're the only suspect." He grabbed a washcloth from the basket next to the sink and wet it under the tap, then stood in front of her. "Show me the injury."

She hesitated, her lips pressing together in a firm line.

He handed her the cloth and turned to leave. "Fine. Have it your way. Good luck spotting any glass that might still be embedded on your own."

"Wait." When he turned around, she huffed and stuck out her left foot. "Here."

Finley projected an impregnable suit of armor around her that made her imposing. Larger than life. Even when they had been together, Finley always seemed to have descended from a higher, more exalted plane than where he and other mere mortals dwelled. But when he took the wet cloth back from her and knelt before her, he realized with an electric shock that he had forgotten some things about her after all. Like how without the sharply tailored suits and shoes with heels so tall and thin they could double as weapons, she was rather petite in build. The contrast between the untouchable Finley he'd built up in his mind over the years versus the all-too-vulnerable woman before him made him dizzy.

But only for a second.

He ran the cloth over the cut. Finley inhaled a sharp hiss, her foot trembling in his grasp. The glass had sliced deep, but the wound was clean and free of additional shards. He threw a quick glance up at her. She was stone-faced, her gaze landing anywhere but on him. "You'll live," he said, his voice rough.

"Thank you once more for your keenly observed medical assessment." She kept her face turned away.

"There are bandages under the sink." He rose, then pointed at her. "Don't move."

She indicated the soaking-wet towel wrapped around her with a sweep of her hand. "And to think I was just about to make my debut on the red carpet."

"Don't try to stand." He found the first aid kit at the back of the sink cabinet. She remained exactly where he had left her, frozen in place. Her knuckles were white from clenching the rolled edge of the tub, their color matching her complexion.

He returned to his kneeling position. "Still don't like the sight of blood, I see."

Her gaze snapped to meet his. It was the first time they made eye contact since he entered the bathroom. "I don't know what you're talking about."

Her words were full of bravado, but she focused on the ceiling as he examined her injured sole, her foot shaking in his grasp. It was yet another reminder that a vulnerable human being existed underneath Finley's highly polished surface. A reminder he didn't need, damn it. He was perfectly fine thinking of Finley as a glossy two-dimensional image designed to dazzle and seduce but lacking anything resembling real depth.

"No, of course you don't. There's another reason why you're holding on to the tub as if you are about to faint. Or as if it were a wooden door floating in the ocean and the *Titanic* just sank." He threw her a brief grin. Finley used to tease him about his lack of film knowledge. He mentally thanked his sisters for forcing him to watch that movie with them on a rainy Sunday afternoon.

"You're the one who told me not to move."

"When have you ever done what people tell you? Least of all me." He finished bandaging her foot and sat back on his heels. "Done. It's safe to look now. Or to go back in the water, as the case may be."

"That's *Jaws*. You're mixing up your pop culture history references. Some things never change." But her hands relaxed, her shoulders visibly falling to settle in their usual position. Her foot stopped trembling and pink bloomed on what had been ashen cheeks.

Yes, Finley was all too human. And an attractive one at that. One who had a power like no other to make his blood boil—but not in anger. No, his last argument with Finley left him cold and desolate. But passion… She was the only person he'd met so far who could instinctively find his ignition switch, rendering him hot and hard and lacking in conscious thought in seconds flat. Just one sideways flick of her glance and—

He made the mistake of looking up. Her dark eyes glittered in the dim light. Her full lips parted as she inhaled. And he was suddenly, intimately aware they were alone in the ranch house.

The steam in the air wrapped around them, narrowing the world to Finley and him. He still cradled her foot in his hands. It would be all too easy to slide those hands up to her calves. And then higher. The towel barely reached the tops of her thighs. She wore nothing underneath. In a different time, a different place, her legs would fall open for him. He would just have to lean forward and his mouth would be perfectly positioned to...

He swallowed. Then he stood, both to regain his equilibrium and to remove the glistening, tempting skin from his gaze.

"Not everyone had the leisure time as kids to watch old movies around the clock." He fell back into their old argument as if they had last discussed his abysmal knowledge of pop culture and film history fifteen minutes ago instead of fifteen years, and some of the swirling tension dissipated.

Some.

"It's adorable you continue to think that's how I grew up." She wriggled her toes on her hurt foot. "Everything works."

"Did you expect otherwise?"

She threw him a look from under her eyelashes. Now that her foot was bandaged, he could see her armor clinking back into place. Walling her away from his grasp, as before. "You always did like playing the good Boy Scout, so no. I didn't expect you to rub salt in the wound. Literally, that is. Metaphorically, that's a different story."

Metaphorically, Finley's expression promised to rub salt mixed with lemon juice into any emotional wound of his she could find. Not that they were hidden. Finley brought all the old hurts to the surface.

"No. That's more your style. No pain, no gain, especially when it comes to other people, right?" He turned to leave. "You're welcome, by the way," he threw at her over his shoulder.

"I was the one enjoying a nice, leisurely, *solo*—" she stressed the last word "—bath when you barged in and everything went to hell as a result. I could've bandaged my own injury."

"Of course. Once you woke up after fainting at the sight of blood. Hitting your head on the stone tile in the process." He reached for the door handle.

She huffed loudly behind his back. "What are you doing here, Will? This was supposed to be Grayson and Nelle's honeymoon. You were not invited along."

That paused him in his tracks. Now that Finley mentioned it, he did recall Lauren mentioning the ranch house would be occupied by guests. He'd been so eager to get out of the rain and get some rest, he didn't question his decision to exit the freeway. He turned to face Finley. "Running Coyote belongs to Reid Begaye."

"I'm aware of that fact," she said tartly, appearing fully recovered from her earlier bout of light-headedness. She perched on the wide edge of the tub as if it were the throne of her own personal country. "Reid is good friends with Nelle. He offered the ranch to Grayson and her as a honeymoon location. When they decided to go elsewhere, they transferred his offer to me."

"Reid may be friends with Nelle, but he is my brother-in-law. He recently married my sister Lauren. I was at your brother's wedding because Reid couldn't make it and Lauren didn't want to go alone. You met her, briefly."

Finley's eyes widened. "Oh. I thought maybe she was…"

"My wife or girlfriend?" He shook his head. "Don't have, either." Then he mentally kicked himself. Why did he tell her that? He hastened to add, "I was driving from Napa to Los Angeles. The weather caused backups on the freeway. When I saw the exit for the ranch, I decided to get out of traffic and the rain. I had no idea you were here. Honest."

Finley's unreadable gaze searched his, but then her shoulders relaxed. Just a fraction of an inch.

She opened her mouth to speak, but he cut her off before she could form words. "Don't worry, I'll leave. Give me a few minutes and I'll be back on the road."

She shifted, and then checked to make sure her towel remained in place. "Is it still raining?"

They were both silent for a minute. The sound of water pelting the roof with rapid force filled the room.

"Sounds like we should start building an ark." She sighed. "Reid will cut off his generous support of Nelle's nonprofit if you leave and hydroplane into a ten-car pileup. You need to stay."

"Not if it will make you uncomfortable." It was one thing to know Finley and he happened to be at the same wedding, surrounded by crowds of merrymakers. It was another to be aware they were the only two people in residence at the ranch, late at night.

She rolled her eyes. "You already did your good deed for the day and rescued the fair maiden—twice if we include Napa—so quit the noble martyr act. This place is large enough to be a boutique hotel. I doubt we'll even see each other."

He wasn't thrilled with the idea of getting back on the dark, slick roads himself. He'd just have to take some of the emergency sleeping aids he had on hand for travel so thoughts of Finley and rehashing how that summer had gone so terribly wrong wouldn't keep him awake. "If you're sure." He hesitated, knowing he was about to pry, but decided to do it, anyway. "I hope no one will mind I stayed here alone with you."

"If you're trying to ask if you need to worry about a jealous partner somewhere out there in the rain, the answer is no, I don't have one. And I'm all out of engraved invitations, so you'll just have to settle for my word that I'm okay with the situation."

Finley was right. Running Coyote had more than enough space for two people. There were plenty of other bedrooms. The guest suite had the most amenities, as Reid and Lauren kept it stocked for spur-of-the-moment company, but the other rooms were luxurious by any standard. The offer certainly beat spending the night fighting the rain and the other cars on the freeway. "Fine. I have to leave first thing to make my meeting in LA as it is."

"I'll be sleeping in." She rose from her seat on the

side of the tub. Her posture was straight, her head held high, but he noticed she did not put weight on her injured foot.

He also noticed the curve of her calves, the long length of her thighs. The juncture between her legs, just hidden from view by the towel. He shifted. His jeans remained tight in the crotch, and not because they were still soaked from the rain.

Finley cleared her throat. "Now that we've established whether you are staying or not, I would like to slip into something a bit more…dry."

Heat settled on his cheeks. "Of course. Sorry again for disturbing you. Good night."

"I doubt we'll run into each other in the morning. So—" Something bright flashed in her gaze. "Farewell, Will."

Her words struck a target he wasn't previously aware he possessed. No, he had no intention of seeing Finley again. He didn't want her phone number. He wasn't planning on friending her on social media, not that he used it much. His assistant ran all the accounts the production company set up for him to use during the filming and promotion of the TV series. The TV series, which would lead to finally finding his perfect life partner if all went to plan. A partner who would be the opposite of Finley in every way.

But the finality of her tone took him aback, to his displeased surprise. She was just as adamant as he was about returning to the state of radio silence between them, apparently. Her words shouldn't make his throat tight and his stomach twinge. But they did.

He focused on the last thing she said. Farewell. As in "fare well"—in other words, be well. Not good-bye, which had no implied wish for his future health.

Will liked numbers. Coding made sense to him. He could fix almost anything in coding by understanding the structure. Language wasn't as cut and dried as ones and zeros. But like numbers, words carried meaning.

"Fare well, Finley."

He shut the bathroom door behind him.

Seven

The noise woke Finley up. Loud and immediate and strong, the roar shook the walls as if a freight train had slammed into the ranch house. The windows rattled. The bed bumped the wall. Finley sat up, wide awake despite having just fallen into a fitful sleep.

The room was dark. So dark, she blinked a few times to make sure her eyes were open. At first, she had no idea where or even when she was. She'd been dreaming of that long-ago summer in Washington, DC, the details vivid and specific. Dreaming of her first meeting with Will.

They were both college interns on Capitol Hill, enrolled in a program that allowed them to earn credits for the spring semester of their senior year while working. She attended a private women's college in the Bay Area. He was finishing up at the University of Illinois Chicago. They met at a rowdy mixer at a bar in Georgetown. She was the ringleader of the party, dancing on tables, urging others to join her, enjoying her first month of being twenty-one. He was in the corner, absorbed in reading a policy paper.

At first, he annoyed her. How dare he ignore her and her friends? They were fun, something he emphatically wasn't. She decided to interrupt his intent perusal, draping herself across the back of his chair and criticizing his paper over his shoulder. They quickly got into a battle of wits over the pros and cons of the paper's subject. Their conversation lasted all night and into the early morning hours, Finley's friends leaving one by one with puzzled stares on their faces. When she discovered he hadn't seen that summer's blockbuster movie, she insisted he go with her to see it the next day.

She couldn't remember the name of the film. She could describe every inch of stubble on his cheeks, how his lips felt against hers. In her dream, he'd been leaning over her, his gray-blue eyes black in the cinema's darkness, staring at her like she was something precious and rare…

Another rattle and the windows vibrated. Her heart beat rapidly. Her throat was dry. She used every breathing exercise in her repertoire to bring her harsh panting under control so her ears could strain to listen for additional noises.

All was now quiet. But what had happened? An earthquake? She scanned the room, looking for the safest place under which to shelter if the ground shook again, and reached for her phone. She rolled her eyes at the low-battery indicator. Great. She'd plugged the phone into the charger, but she must not have plugged the charger into the wall. A half-hour encounter with Will Taylor and she was so flustered, she forgot the most basic routines of modern life.

The screen read five o'clock in the morning. She quickly scrolled through news alerts and her social media accounts. No reports of earthquakes in the Santa Barbara area from official sources. That meant she didn't need to worry about aftershocks—or worry that an even bigger jolt was on its way. Her heart rate returned to something approaching normal.

The torrential storm, on the other hand, was receiving plenty of attention around the internet. The past summer had seen an increase in brush fires, leaving the landscape denuded and barren. People were speculating about the effect of so much rain on hillsides that no longer possessed the vegetation to anchor the topsoil and prevent landslides.

She swung her feet out of bed. Whatever had woken her up may not be an earthquake, but it made a very solid building shake. She needed to know what caused it, to assure herself she didn't need to evacuate to somewhere safer.

Besides, she should check on Will. Just to make sure he was okay, of course. Nelle would never speak to her again if she allowed Reid Begaye's brother-in-law to suffer. No matter how much Finley wanted him to—no.

She didn't want Will to suffer. On the contrary.

She shook her head. Now was not the time for messy thoughts. They'd have to wait. She felt around for her running shoes next to the bed and slipped them on. Then she flipped the bedside lamp's switch.

Her room remained dark.

Her pulse sped up again. And went into triple time when a knock sounded at her door. "Finley? You okay?"

She jerked the door open before he finished speaking. Will stood in the dark sitting room, an opaque outline blending into shadows. She could barely see him. But she felt his presence. "I'm fine. You?"

"Fine."

"What caused that noise? I thought the windows were going to come out of their frames."

"Earthquake?"

"No reports of tremors on social media."

"Power is out. Generator didn't kick in for some reason."

"I noticed."

Will didn't immediately respond but she heard his breathing, steady and low. The sound gave her a reassurance she didn't realize she needed, but was grateful for. "I'll take a look around the house, see if I can find what's wrong with the generator," he said.

"I'm coming with you." She closed the bedroom door behind her. "There has to be a phone landline in this place."

Will shook his head. "Reid got rid of the landline a while ago—said the nuisance calls disturbed his peace—but the CB radio in the kitchen should work. Runs on batteries."

"Good. We'll go to the kitchen."

"I'll go," he reiterated. "Stay here. You've already injured your ankle and foot. I'd hate to see what you hurt next."

"First, if I want to come with you, that's up to me, not you. Second, I put on sensible shoes. See?" She turned on her phone's flashlight app and shined it on her legs and feet.

Too late, she realized she was wearing a thin T-shirt that barely covered the tops of her thighs. Will's gaze dropped, and then lingered.

Her legs always were one of her best physical assets.

She refused to be embarrassed. Besides, the T-shirt concealed more than the towel had last night. And it wasn't as if Will hadn't explored every millimeter of her, with his touch as well as his sight. She might be rounder here, more angular there, but she never cared what the beauty media said was the socially acceptable standard for women's appearance and she wasn't going to start now. She certainly wasn't going to play coy in front of Will. And if seeing her reminded him he'd once had her, all of her, and chosen to walk away—so be it.

Still, she turned the light off, plunging them both back into the darkness. "My phone didn't charge. Need to conserve battery," she said, and then wondered why she was explaining. She cleared her throat and found her best businesslike voice, the one she used to communicate with interns and staff members and nosey journalists. "Want to use your phone?"

"Mine is completely dead. It didn't charge, either. Storm must have knocked the power out after we went to bed. But I can get us to the kitchen without light. Since you won't stay here."

"We don't know what caused the noise. And if this were a horror movie and you left me behind, I'd be the first one picked off by the serial killer and it would be your fault." Actually, the young adults who sneaked away to have sex would be the first ones murdered, but she didn't want to bring that up to Will for very good reasons.

"This is why I don't watch films. Fine." He grabbed her left hand.

"Hey!" She snatched her hand back. Her skin burned where it had briefly slid against his.

He sighed. "It's dark. There's no power. You can stay here where it's safe, no serial killers, until the sun comes up. Or we hold hands so I can make sure you don't trip and harm yourself."

"Of course there aren't any serial killers. I'm just saying if you watched movies like nearly every other human on this planet, you would recognize the situation." She steeled herself, then placed her hand in his.

His grip was warm, and strong, and infinitely comforting.

And arousing. She muttered a prayer of thanks under her breath for the darkness. Not only did she have a reason to hold on to Will, but her tightly pebbled nipples, pushing against the thin material of her shirt, were hidden from his view.

She never would have found the kitchen without using the map of the house Nelle had provided, but Will moved confidently through the corridors and connecting atriums, his guidance firm and unerring. It was even more of a turn-on. When did Will become so, well, sure of himself?

Or maybe... Maybe he always was, and she had been too preoccupied with her own issues to recognize that not all strength was loud and flashy, like Barrett's. Some strength was quiet. Thoughtful. Measured. Like Will's.

And she clung to that strength when she heard staticky voices in the distance. "What was that?"

"Still not serial killers. It's the CB radio. Someone is calling the house."

"Oh." But when she would drop his hand, his fingers tightened on hers.

When they entered the kitchen, the words became clearer, repeated every minute or so. "Running Coyote, this is base camp. Come in. Can you hear us? Over."

Will picked up the radio from its alcove. "This is Running Coyote. Tim, that you?"

There was silence on the other end. Then a burst of static. "This is Tim Stern. Who's this?"

"It's Will Taylor. Lauren's brother. Long story, but I'm here with Finley Smythe. What's going on?"

"Hey, Will. We didn't know you were coming. Is Ms. Smythe okay?"

Finley took the radio from Will and depressed the button to talk. "I'm good. Did you hear the noise? It shook the house. Everyone okay where you are?"

"We sure did hear it. We're all fine down here. But listen, it appears that noise was a good-sized portion of the hillside coming down. Mudslide."

Right. Her speculation about the effect of so much rain at one time on the parched earth had been spot-on. "How bad was it? I hope no one is hurt."

"That's the good news. No one was injured. And as far as we can tell, no buildings were affected, either."

Finley sank against the kitchen counter. Mudslides could be devastating. And fatal, if evacuation warnings didn't come in time or weren't heeded. "That's great."

"But…" Tim hesitated. "The road to the ranch? That's the bad news."

Will took the radio from Finley's suddenly nerveless grasp. "What are you saying? The road is gone?"

"Not gone," Tim said. "Still there. But buried."

"How buried?" Icicles dripped from Will's words.

"The boys are still out there, taking a look. But from what they've radioed me, I'd say you better plan on staying put for at least several days."

"I can't do that," Will stated.

Finley took the radio back from him and spoke to Tim. "There has to be another way to leave the ranch."

"Well, sure, if you like hiking and camping and you have a few days. There are some excellent trails nearby as we're surrounded by a national forest, but it will take you a while to arrive at anything resembling civilization. Might find coyotes, though. Cougars, too."

"Cougars. Awesome." She stared at Will. This

wasn't happening. She was not stuck at a ranch in the midst of nowhere with him.

"Don't forget coyotes," Will said under his breath.

"How could I forget? The ranch is named after them. Running ones, even." She pushed the talk button on the radio. "When can we expect you at the house, Tim?"

"Maybe on Friday, if all goes well. Depends on when we can get a cleanup crew out here and how fast they go."

Finley blinked. "Today is Monday. I was thinking lunchtime."

"Sorry, I didn't make myself clear. The landslide took out the road to the ranch between base camp— that's what we call the compound where Mariam and me and the boys who work on the ranch bunk—and the main house. Afraid you'll have to be on your own for a while. Hey, it's pretty provident Will showed up, isn't it? We were worried about you being all alone."

No, she did not consider it provident Will was there. At all.

Will took the radio back. "When did you say the road would be passable again? Friday?"

"I might be able to make it up there by Friday if we get enough of a path cleared, but I was thinking of walking or riding one of the horses. Cars, who knows? Depends on what other damage was caused by the storm, and who needs the cleanup crew the most."

Will nodded. Outwardly he appeared calm, as if he was merely discussing the weather. But the cords in his neck pulsed, a sign he was agitated. Funny, how details she once thought were lost forever to the past were now fresh and bright.

"Speaking of," Tim continued, "I'm doubly glad you're there, Will, because I need you to check on the horses in the upper barn. Most of the animals are down here with us at the main stables, but we left Trudy and Ranger near the house for Ms. Smythe to ride. You good with feeding them and making sure they're okay until I can get up there?"

The cords in Will's neck tightened. "Sure."

"Mariam says there is enough food stocked in the kitchen to last you for a good while. You two will be dandy."

Dandy was not the word Finley would use to describe the situation. Her stomach roiled.

"I hope she's not including the contents of the refrigerator. Electricity is out and the generator didn't come on," Will said.

Tim sighed. "I told Reid that generator system was useless. We have engineers scheduled to come out and look at it. Oh, and you might want to conserve water as the well pump house is on the same system. But there should be enough in the storage tank to last you until the power is back on."

Will stared at Finley. She stared back. "What are the chances of having the power restored soon?" Will asked.

His only answer was a burst of static. Then Tim's voice returned. "Sorry, folks, I got to run. The boys discovered some storm damage to the corrals, and I need to take a look. I'll get back to you soon." The radio went silent.

Great. No power, limited water, and no way to leave the ranch. With her only companion the man who'd demonstrated to her true love was a farce.

The sun had come up during their conversation with Tim, but the light was dull as a steady drizzle cast a misty filter over the landscape outside the windows. Heavy gray clouds pressed down on what Finley assumed would be an impressive vista under other circumstances. Obviously, escaping Will by spending the day basking by the pool was not a current option.

She picked up her phone. The battery symbol remained depressingly low. She checked her email, reading only the subject lines. Grayson and Nelle had landed in London: good. Her car was due for service: delete. Sadiya had an update on Erica O'Connell's book… Her finger hovered over the email, then clicked Open.

Sadiya's message wasn't long. Erica's memoir was still officially under wraps, but journalists were on the scent. Sadiya was fielding phone calls by the hour. She urged Finley to stay put wherever she was.

Finley sighed. That wouldn't be too hard. She returned to her email inbox, only for the screen to go black as the battery finally gave out.

The noise of pot lids falling to the terra-cotta-tiled floor caused her to glance up. Will was opening cupboards and drawers in the expansive kitchen. And the daylight showed her what she had been too stressed to notice earlier: he wore only beat-up sneakers and a pair of midnight blue boxers, low slung on narrow hips. His back muscles flexed as he rummaged through their contents and her gaze was caught, like a moth drunk on candlelight.

Finley believed she had filled her visual reference banks with images of a half-dressed Will the night before. But she'd been in pain—and damn it, he was right that the sight of blood was not high on her list of favorite things—and focused on appearing poised in front of him. Now she realized just how many details she had missed. Like the way his hair was just long enough to form perfect curls at the nape of his neck. The way his torso narrowed from broad shoulders to slim hips. The flawless globes of his ass as he bent down to look inside a cabinet…

He swung his head and looked at her from over his shoulder. A knowing smile spread over his face. *Busted.*

She cleared her throat. "So. I guess neither of us is leaving anytime soon."

"I'm not hearing you complaining." He smirked before standing up and opening another cabinet. Was it her imagination or did he flex his biceps more than was necessary?

His smug tone was not something she conjured up. *Face facts, Finley.* If she had been in charge of the universe, she would never have encountered Will Taylor again. She would have been perfectly content going to her grave without knowing fifteen years of additional maturity only made him more attractive.

But she wasn't in charge. And fate, always a fickle

devil who loved to laugh at people's best intentions, had other plans for her. Therefore, she had at least two choices. One, draw a line down the middle of the ranch house and declare the other side off-limits. Then lock herself into the guest suite and venture to the kitchen for food only when she was confident Will was occupied elsewhere. Ignore him, acting as if she was the only resident of the house.

Or two…acknowledge that she and Will were alone, together, and wipe the smirk off his face by beating him at the game of who could make the other sweat the most. And if history was anything to go on, they could make each other sweat quite a lot.

But this time, her heart would be locked away. This time, she would be firmly in control. Extravagant promises would not soften her into thinking he loved her. She would not be fooled again.

She would have her way with him—it went without saying he would have a good time as well—and then walk away. Match point to her.

She liked games. She especially liked winning them. And the bulge in his jeans the night before demonstrated he was not wholly indifferent, giving her an advantage. She ignored inconvenient details, like his presence jumpstarting her sorely neglected libido, roaring to sudden life.

Kicking off her running shoes, she hopped onto the stone slab counter next to him. "What are you looking for?" she purred.

"Taking stock of our supplies." He motioned at

her. "Move to the left so I can get into that cupboard underneath you?"

"Of course." She elaborately wriggled her rear along the cool smooth surface. Her T-shirt rode up even farther, exposing more of her thighs.

Will's smirk disappeared. His expression remained impassive as he squatted down and opened one of the doors. She kept her right leg in his view. When it came to Will, she had two potent weapons in her arsenal, and she intended to use them.

She swung her uninjured right foot and her toes briefly grazed the tops of his thigh. "See anything interesting? Anything you'd like to have…later?"

The tips of his ears turned red, a sign she knew well. She smiled. Winning was going to be far easier than she'd hoped for. She brushed his thigh again, lingering a few seconds longer. "Or are you…hungry…now?"

He stood up, so fast she didn't have time to react and rearrange her legs so he wasn't directly between them. She scooted back, but quickly ran out of counter. He leaned forward. Her heart pounded as he braced his hands on either side of her.

His eyes were level with hers, so close the navy rim outlining his gray-blue pupils was discernible. His breath tickled her skin, raising teeny goose bumps. She could incline her head, just a hair, and she would know if he remembered exactly how she liked to be kissed.

Their gazes locked. The morning air was chilly, but she was hot. Surface-of-the-sun hot. Her lips needed moisture and she licked them. Will's gaze dropped, tracing the path of her tongue. Then he leaned forward even farther. Their foreheads almost touched. Her nipples tightened as a rush of heat settled low in her belly. She closed her eyes, her mouth slightly open...

"You're still in the way." Will straightened up and moved to the section of the kitchen farthest from her.

She swallowed, attempting to regain control and flush the desire out of her system. Score one point for Will, but the game clock was far from running out. Plenty of opportunities to win this thing. "Sorry." She wasn't. Not at all. "What's convenient for breakfast?"

Will closed a drawer with more force than necessary. "Convenient? Nothing about this is convenient."

"Maybe not for you," she said, thinking of Sadiya's email. "You said something last night about a meeting. An important one?"

"Yes."

She raised her eyebrows in inquiry, but he apparently had finished speaking. "I see your conversational skills have atrophied."

She hopped off the counter and began to explore the butler's pantry adjacent to the kitchen, which Will hadn't looked in yet. She hated to admit it, but his Boy Scout instinct to assess their supplies was a damn good one. Especially since the kitchen's large, eight-burner professional-grade range was electric. As was the microwave, of course.

"I'm not your first choice of human beings with whom to be stranded and you're certainly not mine, but here we are," she called out, rummaging through a treasure trove of small appliances, all requiring a working power outlet. "We might as well make the most of it."

When several minutes passed without a response from her companion, she poked her head out of the pantry. "Will?"

The kitchen was empty.

She sagged against the pantry's floor-to-ceiling cabinets. Great. But wasn't this what she ultimately wanted? A life free of Will Taylor? Why was she upset if Will decided to keep as much space as possible between them until they were able to leave Running Coyote?

The sound of a throat being cleared got her attention. Will was just outside the pantry door. He'd thrown on well-worn jeans and a black sweatshirt. With his left hand, he held out a men's-sized long-sleeved flannel shirt. "It's freezing in here," he said. "Don't want you to catch a cold."

She blinked at him but slipped on the offered garment. The shirt was long enough on her to be worn as a dress and she sank into its enveloping warmth. It smelled like him, too. She fought the urge to deeply inhale.

So strange how, of all the senses, smell conjured the clearest, most detailed memories. She'd tripped down memory lane so often in the last few days, the path was well worn. But the shirt's scent, indescribable with words but immediately recognizable as him, caused vivid images to tumble in front of her eyes. Will, smiling at her as he handed her a drink at a congressional intern party. Will, stammering as he asked her out following their movie date. Will, slowly unbuttoning her shirt, kissing each inch of skin he exposed as if she were something precious and wondrous...

"Thank you," she finally remembered to say.

"We don't have access to a doctor or pharmacy. And with your recent track record of falls and cuts, better not risk illness." His tone was deadpan, but she saw the glimmer of humor deep in his gaze.

She folded her arms across her chest. "Does this usually work for you, rescuing women who have no need of your assistance?"

He threw a pointed glance at her injured foot and ankle.

Time to change the subject. "I'll take care of the horses. You can figure out breakfast."

He shook his head. "I told Tim I'd feed the horses. Why don't you go back to your room. Get some rest. You woke up pretty early."

She laughed. If he wanted to put space between them, he'd have to try harder than that. "Rest for what? My strenuous day of being trapped on this ranch? Besides, can you even identify one end of a horse from the other?"

"I'm assuming they eat with the end that has a mouth."

"Not an answer."

He walked to the closest kitchen counter and busied himself with opening a loaf of bread and taking a jar from a nearby shelf. "Peanut butter okay? Be warned now—you don't have many choices."

She watched him slather a bread slice with the thick spread. "Peanut butter sandwich. That takes me back. I haven't had one since the internsh—" She bit back the rest of her words. "Since forever."

Will handed her a completed sandwich along with a ripe banana taken from the fruit bowl on the counter. "Too bad. You used to devour them."

Their gazes met. Finley could only hold his for a second before she dropped hers to focus on her food. "I used to devour a lot of things, like ramen and microwave popcorn." *And Will.* "I'm guessing those are off the menu. Since we don't have a working microwave."

"Don't worry. You don't need to pretend you're one of the common people now. You're safe from supermarket specials." He bit into his own sandwich.

Her mouth went dry, but the crunchy peanut butter was not the culprit. "What do mean, pretend?"

His shoulders tensed and he put the rest of his sandwich down. "Forget I said anything. I'm going to feed the horses."

She followed him to the adjacent breakfast room and out the French doors that led to a sprawling flagstone terrace. Beyond, the lush green lawn sloped down to the Olympic-sized pool and the built-in cabanas surrounding it. At any other time, she would admire the view of the jagged hills wreathed in fog and dark clouds, but now all she saw was red. "Pretending would be continuing to act like passing acquaintances who share a history of polite nods and nothing more. If you have something to say to me, then say it."

"Stay in the house where it's dry, Finley."

"Stop giving me orders, Will."

He strode across the terrace until it ended and then took a path off to the left. "I wouldn't give you an order. You do what you want. You always do."

He muttered the last three words, but the wind carried them to her as clearly as if he had said them in her ear. She hurried after him. "And what is that supposed to mean?"

Will picked up his steps. She'd have to break into a trot to keep up. And while she would rather die than admit her pain to him, her injured foot and the ankle she had twisted were in less-than-optimal shape. The chilly mist-filled air raised goose bumps on her bare legs, also reminding her she wasn't dressed for a visit to a barn.

She stopped and turned around to reenter the house.

But not because Will told her to. And he was not off the hook. She was going to make Will explain himself. And remember he once couldn't get enough of her. But this time, she'd be the one walking away with her heart intact and he'd be the one left on his knees, gasping for oxygen.

She loved it when a plan came together.

Eight

Will heard Finley open the door to the barn—who else would it be?—but he stayed where he was, staring at the array of bales and containers in the stable's feed room. Not that he was surprised Finley wasn't sensible enough to stay inside the house where it was relatively warm. Finley never could resist having the last word. And once upon a time her last words made him laugh, so he was happy to let her have the final say.

But that was then.

Now? Will was no longer ensorcelled by Finley's allure. He was not going to fall under her spell again. Not after causing his heart a bruising case of whiplash when she turned cold and cutting without any advance warning. She could swing her impossibly long and luscious legs in his line of sight all she wanted.

Sure, his body reacted to her. He was only human. And Finley was everything he found desirable. He still had the same effect on her, too. Her eyes were normally the color of a glass of whiskey held up to the sunlight, a warm amber brown. But when Finley was aroused, her eyes became deep, dark pools. He could have drowned in her gaze when they were in the kitchen earlier.

He looked down and realized he had filled the horse's feed buckets with the wrong mixture. Cursing himself for letting Finley affect him, he threw out the contents and started all over.

This couldn't have happened at a worse time. The meeting in Los Angeles was happening in three hours. Obviously, showing up for it was in the realm of science fiction. He'd asked Tim via the CB radio to call the series producers and make Will's excuses, but he'd learned from experience the Screenweb executives were prickly, demanding and allergic to compromises. He only hoped when they heard a natural disaster was behind his absence from the crucial kickoff meeting, they would agree to continue with the original production timeline. Ji-Hoon deserved to have his dream come true, and they were in a battle against time.

His mentor was the only reason Will had said yes when the production company knocked on his door, seeking the next big reality dating series. He certainly didn't need the additional income. Even before the EverAftr app had become a hit, he held the patents on several innovative pieces of software that made streaming services and ISPs more secure, valued at millions apiece to the companies that purchased them. Savvy investing had caused his net worth to grow, to the point that if EverAftr were to disappear tomorrow, it would barely be a blip in his portfolio.

If he'd told his twenty-one-year-old self that he would be featured on *Silicon Valley Weekly*'s list of top tech execs to watch…maybe his younger self wouldn't have so readily accepted the label of "not good enough" and slunk out of Washington, DC, giving up his original goal of working for the Justice Department. Instead of law school, he'd gone back to his high school hobby of playing with software code and turned it into a career.

That choice hadn't worked out so bad, had it?

Focus on what matters now, he admonished himself. The company. The television series. At the kick-off meeting he was currently missing, they were supposed to discuss his potential matches for the first episode. He'd filled out his EverAftr questionnaires just before leaving for Napa, stressing his ideal qualities in partner, including constancy, steadiness and an even temper.

If only the perfect partner he'd described didn't appear boring and colorless now that he'd spent time with Finley again.

A horse snorted, breaking his reverie. He went to the doorway and saw Finley standing in front of a stall with "Trudy" written in erasable marker on its metal nameplate, stroking the nose of the buff-colored mare. She'd exchanged her running shoes for boots and changed into jeans that cupped her ass in ways that should be illegal.

Tucked into those jeans, she still wore his shirt.

"Aren't you a pretty girl," Finley cooed to Trudy. "I bet you're wondering why the nice man is standing in the room with your food instead of giving the food to you." She looked over at him. "Need a hand? I happen to know my way around a stable."

"I've got it, thanks." Of course she was familiar with horses. All his success, yet when he was with Finley he turned back into the kid who had never visited an art museum or seen professional live theater before meeting her. Uninformed. Unsophisticated. And in this case, unfamiliar with large hooved animals and their care and feeding.

She nodded. "Okay. Hay is in the greenish bales, by the way. The straw-colored bales are, well, straw."

"You're very helpful," he said dryly.

Her smile was dazzling. "Always."

After much comparison of labels with the instructions to ensure he had the right combination this time, he portioned the grains and roughage for each horse into their respective buckets and carried them out of the room. The dusty smell of cut alfalfa and the warm scent of horse surrounded him. He never thought stables could feel cozy—well, he never thought of stables at all—but although the weather outside was dark and foreboding, inside all appeared light and inviting.

Or maybe that was due to Finley. She'd entered Trudy's stall and was brushing the mare's coat with something resembling circles of jagged metal. "That looks more like a torture instrument," he said by way of greeting, opening the stall door to fill the feeder.

"Are you worried I'll use it on you later? Or are you hoping?" She wagged her eyebrows, making him laugh despite his best efforts not to. "This is a currycomb. Because your paddock is full of mud and you got it all over yourself, didn't you, beauty?" She stroked Trudy's nose, long, sweeping caresses the mare appeared to enjoy, judging by the way she nuzzled Finley.

It was ridiculous to be jealous of an animal. Will stomped over to the other occupied stall, this one marked "Ranger," and dumped the contents of the bucket in the appropriate place. The chestnut gelding ignored him in favor of his food. "You have the right idea, buddy. Take care of number one. Don't care about others."

But when he left Ranger's stall, Finley was nowhere to be found. He hadn't heard her leave, so she had to be around somewhere. "Finley?"

"In Trudy's paddock," came her distant voice.

He pushed Trudy's stall door open. On the other side of the enclosed space, there was a passage to a small dirt area covered by an overhang to protect it from the elements, and beyond that a fenced-in grassy expanse. Finley stood with Trudy where the grass began, nose to nose, as if they were communing. Then Finley took an apple out of her shirt's front pocket and, taking the first bite, she held out the rest to the horse on her flat palm. Trudy delicately ate the offering, and then sauntered to the far side of the paddock to supplement her breakfast, ignoring the humans in her space. Finley watched the mare go.

Will set out to meet her. As he drew closer, he realized he'd never seen Finley so…unguarded. Her shoulders were relaxed, her hands loose at her sides. The smirk that seemed to have taken up permanent residence on her lips was gone, replaced by a genuine smile.

Even in their most passionate encounters, he'd always known she was holding something back, giving him access to her body but not to the deepest corners of her soul. Now? He caught a glimpse of what she'd previously hidden from him.

She turned her head as he approached. Her sharp, teasing expression returned as her posture straightened and her arms folded over her chest. "Did you feed Ranger?" she called out.

The moment was over. The sting of disappointment caused his steps to falter, just for a beat.

"He's also a horse," she clarified when he reached her side. "Long nose, tail, four legs."

"I figured that out, thanks." He nodded at Trudy. "You two seem to be getting along well."

Her gaze softened as she watched the mare. "My mother loved horses. I grew up around them."

She did? "I didn't know that."

She glanced at him. "We didn't exactly spend our time in soul-baring conversations."

No. They'd used their time for other activities. "Still surprised you didn't say anything."

She laughed, if the harsh exhalation of air could be

called that. "Oh, I'd given up my equestrian dreams by then. I won several jumping competitions as a child. But after my mom died and it became obvious I wasn't talented enough to compete at an elite level, Barrett decided horses were a waste of money and time and that was that." She shrugged. "I moved on."

When she broke up with Will, she'd dismissed their relationship with much the same words: "The internship program is over, so time to move on. We're done." He had been in too much shock—too much agony—to note anything other than her casual dismissal of what had been the most transcendent summer of his life.

He wondered—had deep grooves been etched around her lips then as they were now? Had the same opaque shutters slammed down over her gaze, rendering her true emotions unreadable? If he'd paid closer attention, maybe he would remember.

Then with a blink, her expression smoothed into her usual smirk. She closed the space between them, glancing up at him from under lowered lashes. "But I still enjoy riding." Her voice took on a husky timbre that put his nerve endings on alert. "Perhaps we would both enjoy getting back into the saddle."

"I don't ride."

She smiled. A wicked smile, full of heat and sin. "That's not what I remember. I recall you are quite the…passionate…rider. Endurance for hours, until we were both spent."

God help him, he was hard. Hard and aching, and just from a few whispered words—plus the images his memory supplied to accompany them.

Finley's gaze sparkled as her grin deepened. She knew what she was doing to him. She always knew.

With supreme effort, his brain wrested control from his cock. "I'm returning to the house."

He strode toward the gate that would give him the fastest exit from the paddock. Intent on putting as much space between him and Finley in the shortest amount of time possible, he didn't notice where the rain-soaked grass turned into a large patch of mud. Thick, viscous mud that grabbed his lightweight sneakers and didn't let go when he picked up his right foot.

He stumbled forward. His arms windmilled as he tried to maintain his balance. His other foot slid out from underneath him.

He landed on his hands and knees.

The mud made for a soft if messy landing. His equilibrium was the only thing that took a beating. Well, his equilibrium and his clothes, which would require an industrial-strength cleaning after this. He sat back on his heels, searching for the shoe remaining in the mud.

Finley came running up. Her boots stayed firmly on her feet. No wonder they were obligatory ranch wear. "Are you okay?"

"Nothing hurt but my dignity."

She laughed. "You look like the Abominable Mudman."

"I caught you when you almost fell at the winery. You don't return favors?" Rain dripped from his hair into his eyes. He pushed his hair back, then realized he'd only caked himself with more dirt.

She was laughing so hard, she was nearly doubled over. "Even if I'd been close enough to catch you, what makes you think I could have prevented your fall? We'd both be up to our ears in mud. Nuh-uh."

Her mirth was contagious, damn it. He chuckled. "You don't want to be muddy. But it's funny when other people are?"

"It wouldn't be funny if you were hurt. But since you aren't..." She hiccupped, and wiped tears from her eyes. "Here. To show I'm a good sport, I'll help you up."

She held out her hand. Will took it. She pulled with all her strength.

They both tumbled into mud, Finley landing on top on him. Legs to legs, chest to chest. Finley's soft, warm curves crashed against him. A whoosh of air left him, his breath knocked out in too many ways to count.

Shock made her still. Then after a second, she relaxed into him. His body recognized her instantly. She fit against him as she always did, as if her curves were expressly created to match the planes and dips of his musculature, despite the intervening years. His arms came up to embrace her before he knew what they were doing. He forced them back to his sides.

She lifted her head, her chuckle rumbling through both of them. "You did that on purpose," she stated. "But I agree. Dirty is far more fun when two are involved."

Was that a wriggle to go with her innuendo? Either way, he was aware that only a few layers of fabric separated them. His groin started to make demands his head wasn't sure it could override. "I didn't cause this. *You* didn't dig your feet in and lost your balance."

"Well, you—" She began to laugh again. "Will, you literally have mud in your eye. Or almost. Here, let me." She rolled off him and came to a kneeling position, tugging the shirt she wore free of her jeans. Then, using a clean portion of her shirttails, she leaned down and gently wiped his face. "There."

Their gazes caught. And held. His pulse, never sluggish when Finley was near, beat painfully in his ears. "Thanks."

Mischief danced deep in her eyes. The kind of mischief that once led to sneaking into public gardens after hours and ended with them naked and stifling their screams of pleasure so the security guards wouldn't hear them. "Of course. Who knows what's in this mud? Can't have you getting sick when we're without access to a doctor, remember?"

He remembered, all right. But the memories went much further back than this morning. And he was tired of fighting them off. Tired of acting as if every time Finley was near, his blood didn't turn to gasoline and her teasing smile wasn't an accelerant, lighting him on fire.

Turnabout was fair play, after all.

He rose to his feet, Finley following suit. She looked relatively pristine aside from splatters here and there, but then he'd taken the brunt of their fall.

Mud was everywhere. It clung to his jeans, his shirt, his hair. "Right. Doctors. Is there anywhere else I should be concerned about? Like say, my hands?"

Finley appeared to ponder. "Maybe I should look. In case there's broken skin."

He held them out to her. Her own hands were none too clean, but they both knew his question was only a pretense. Her fingers slowly traced over his palms, his inner wrists, awakening nerve endings he wasn't aware existed. Tiny shock waves reverberated through his system.

She raised her dark gaze to his. "I think they're fine."

"What about my back? It's pretty muddy."

Her slow smile sent a lightning strike of heat to his groin. "I'm happy to examine your backside."

She took her time. And was very thorough. Her hands swept over his shoulders, down his spine, whispered over his buttocks. Her fingers lifted his sweatshirt, explored the area above his jeans waistband, coming close but never quite dipping below it. Who knew that area of skin was one of the body's most erogenous zones? By the time she reappeared in front of him, he was hard and heavy.

"I'm happy to report all appears in fine order." Beneath the mud streaks on her face, her cheeks were flushed crimson. He'd never seen her lovelier.

He nodded, trying to form words. Finally, he forced out, "What about my mouth? I'd hate to ingest something I shouldn't. Since we can't get to the doctor."

Her gaze dropped to the area in question, lingered.

She shook her head slowly, then raised her eyes to his. The mischief was wiped away, replaced by dark flames leaping high. "You're good. But what about mine? Same reason, of course."

Her mouth was…perfect. A full lower lip, soft and pillowy, made to be nibbled on or tugged gently between his teeth. Her upper lip, a cupid's bow of peaks and valleys, wicked in shape and in action. His groin tightened farther at the memory of those lips taking him in, their pressure and pull… He managed to find his voice. "There never was any mud on you, Finley."

She stilled, her eyes losing their light. He frowned but had no time to ask what was wrong before she leaned forward, her hands making fists in his shirt at the shoulders. In her boots she was almost as tall as him, especially since he was still missing a shoe. She raised her head, and that perfect mouth hovered next to his. "Then do something to change that, Will."

He didn't need another invitation.

In Will's life, he'd had three supreme experiences. One, catching a foul ball in the seventh game of the 2016 World Series while cheering his beloved Chicago Cubs to victory. Two, receiving his first software patent. And then there was kissing Finley Smythe for the first time.

Now the list was blown up. Caput. Gone forever. Because nothing could ever, would never, rival kissing Finley in the middle of a horse paddock, covered in mud, the air chilled by mist and wind. Not that he was cold for very long. His blood, already heated, erupted into lava at the first touch of her lips against his.

His tongue played with the seam of her lips, demanding they open to him. Finley made a mewling sound and she crashed into him, her hands tangling in his hair, her tongue coming out to twine and rub against his. Her mouth was hot and wet and she tasted faintly like apple but mostly like Finley, a taste he realized he'd subconsciously missed all these years.

He grabbed her waist, pulling her harder against him. His wandering fingers got her the shirt untucked, so he had access to the warm woman underneath the flannel. His hands splayed against the satin skin of her back, exploring territory that once had been as familiar to him as his own image in a mirror. The knobs of her spine were more pronounced now, the curve of her belly a bit more rounded, but his mind soon stopped the comparison, too busy exploding with the knowledge he was kissing Finley, actually kissing her. Not a dream, not a fantasy.

He ached with want. Finley wrapped her legs around his, pressing her warmth against him. Her hands explored his shoulders, his chest, finding his nipples through his shirt and tweaking them just enough that a groan escaped him. She placed his hands on her breasts, moaning into his mouth and shuddering against him when his fingers and thumbs found the diamond-hard peaks.

She pulled back, just a hand's width. "Let's go back to the house."

He searched her gaze. Her eyes were dark and

wild with passion, yes, but he read something else in her expression.

He read victory.

The fires, burning so high and fierce, swiftly banked.

He hadn't seen Finley in many years, but certain things were seared on his memory and Finley's expressions were among them. Once, she'd finagled an invitation to an exclusive White House gala for him, charming aides and assistants until she found someone willing to put him on the guest list. When he expressed admiration for her ability to cut through barriers thought impregnable, she'd waved a hand. "It's a game."

She had the same expression now.

He stepped back. He dropped his hands to his sides, clenching his fists so he wouldn't give in to the temptation to pull her close, lose himself in the heated flames again.

Confusion chased away the triumph he'd discerned. "Will? What's wrong?" Her smirk appeared. "Because I'm pretty sure we were both enjoying ourselves."

He shook his head. What was he doing? Hadn't he learned the first time? He couldn't be Finley Smythe's diversion when she wanted to amuse herself and nothing better was available to her.

He supposed he should thank her for reminding him why he'd agreed to personally participate in the streaming series based on EverAftr. Not only did he believe in EverAftr's algorithms and ability to match

users with strong possibilities for lifetime partners—
the company's successful matches were too numerous not to be proud of his work—he was growing
tired of coming home to a silent town house. Both
his sisters had recently married and while occasionally Lauren let slip something that raised his doubts
about her relationship with Reid, his sister Claire was
blissfully happy with her wife, Berit. He wanted what
they had for himself.

He could've signed up anonymously for EverAftr,
but his identity was bound to be leaked at one point
or another. He didn't mind the bad press for himself
should a disappointed date leak details to a gossip
website, but the company didn't deserve any potential
negative blowback. It wasn't EverAftr's fault his relationships rarely made it past the three-month mark,
a fact for which he took full blame.

But on the series, his participation would be open
knowledge. His dates would be filmed on camera,
with the participants' full agreement, for the world
to see for themselves. He welcomed the challenge of
proving EverAftr's value in public, standing behind
his company's promise.

Making his mentor's cherished dream come true
was just the compelling cherry on top. Ji-Hoon believed in him when he needed the external valida-
tion the most.

But Finley? After that summer, she dismissed him.
Threw away the offer of his heart and soul. She'd had
bigger goals in her sights, and blithely dumped him
to pursue dreams that didn't include him.

He couldn't fall under her spell again. Yes, he wanted her. Who wouldn't? She was smart and made him laugh and her intoxicating kisses were addicting. He shook with his craving for more.

But he wasn't an impoverished twenty-one-year-old student blinded by her glamour. He had a life. He ran a successful business. People depended on him.

He wanted her, but want wasn't enough. Not with so much else on the line.

"Will?" she repeated. She raised her chin, folding her arms across her chest.

"It's getting colder," he said. He wasn't just referring to the weather. "I'm going to the house to get rid of this mud. And then I need to work. You won't see me for the rest of the day."

"I don't—what the blazing hell, Will? That wasn't a flashlight in your pocket."

She was furious. And with Finley, anger didn't flare red hot. But it burned, in the way frozen metal seared unprotected skin.

"Be honest. For once." He stared her down. "Is this something you really want? Am *I* someone you want? Or are you just bored?"

She didn't say anything. She didn't need to. The forked lightning in her gaze answer enough.

He shook his head. "I find you desirable. I've always found you desirable. I'll find you desirable when we're a hundred and four. But I can't do this again. I'm not and never was your toy."

He opened the gate to the paddock. Closing it behind him, he marched toward the house.

It took every ounce of strength he possessed, even tapping his reserves, not to turn back, pick her up and carry her back with him.

Nine

Finley stared at Will's receding back. Her mouth moved but her brain could not come up with words. And she would be damned if she let Will have the final say. "You better not use up all the water!"

It was the only thing that came to mind. The rest was mixed up in a throbbing miasma of thwarted desire, anger and… Her belly fluttered, and not in the delicious, squeezing way it did when Will was near. This was more like the precursor to the kind of sour stomachache that kept her prone on the sofa.

She'd made an utter fool of herself. But there was one consolation: no one else knew.

Trudy snorted from her corner and looked up at Finley. Finley tended not to anthropomorphize animals, but Trudy's expression clearly read, *That was a fiasco*. Ranger peered over the fence that separated his paddock from Trudy's and tossed his head as if to agree with his stablemate. "Okay," Finley muttered. "You two know."

Nothing to do but wait until Will was safely inside the main house and doing whatever work he thought he could accomplish with a dead phone and no power, and then make her way to the guest suite. Alone. For the rest of however long she was trapped on this forsaken isolated ranch. It was back to her original plan: Operation Will Taylor Does Not Exist.

At least she wouldn't need to worry if the ranch's water heater required electricity to function. She would be taking a cold shower. An unfortunately short one.

The hours dripped by slowly for the rest of the day. Finley took her shower, the bracing water's effect nullified by thoughts of Will's biceps flexing under her grip, his mouth hot and demanding, his denim-clad thigh solid between hers, the rigid shape in his jeans proof he wanted her as much as she wanted him. She picked out a recent bestseller to read from the bookcase in the sitting room of the guest suite, but after reading the first page five times and still not comprehending a word, she decided the problem wasn't the book, it was her inability to concentrate.

She studied the binder outlining all the house amenities since she wasn't about to leave anytime soon, but that failed to eat up much time. Swimming was out of the question, thanks to the rain that decided to make a return visit that afternoon. Thunderstorms were rare in Southern California but not unheard of and with her luck, she couldn't rule out a direct lightning strike on the pool. Hiking was also off the agenda, not only because of the weather but because she wasn't keen on meeting the ranch's namesakes while walking alone.

Next on her list was informing people of her current situation. She ensured the kitchen was empty before entering it, then spoke to Tim via the CB radio, dictating emails for him to send to Sadiya as well as to Grayson and Nelle. Tim informed her the power company was working to restore the ranch's service, but the storm had caused several severe disruptions in the area so he didn't have a time estimate for her. Their conversation took care of another half hour, leaving her the rest of the day to relive what happened in the paddock.

By the time the clock read 11:00 p.m., Finley was all out of ideas to keep herself busy so she wouldn't wallow in thoughts of Will. The house was silent. Granted, the place was so big, Will could be throwing a party for thirty of his noisiest friends and she wouldn't hear them. But it was the type of silence that only came when all the residents were tucked in bed. No doubt Will was sleeping the sleep of angels after their early morning wake-up call, his conscience clear after rejecting her.

No such sleep was in her future. And her stomach, which had been too unsteady to accept much food during the day, loudly reminded her it remained mostly empty. A late night kitchen raid was in order.

Just as she suspected, not a creature was stirring, especially not her ridiculously attractive housemate. She opened and closed cabinets with as much stealth as possible, hoping to avoid yet another main course of peanut butter.

She struck pay dirt behind the sixth door. A bag of large, fluffy marshmallows. Chocolate bars from Italy, in a variety of shades from dark to milk to white. And was that...? Yes! Graham crackers. She gathered her bounty in her arms, intending to return to the guest suite, when she stopped to consider her options.

Standing in the dim, cavernous kitchen, goose bumps had taken over every inch of her exposed skin. If she went back, she could wrap herself in bedding and she'd be warm enough, but wouldn't sitting by a fire be even better? Not to mention she could make real s'mores instead of eating the marshmallows and chocolate cold.

She located metal skewers and napkins, then added a bottle of pinot noir and a corkscrew to her finds before taking them into the living area. She'd noted the wide-tiled fireplace that dominated one wall of the room and the stack of logs piled high next to it when she arrived, along with a basket containing kindling and matches. Finley possessed few practical survival skills—given a choice of vacations, she'd pick a suite at a luxury hotel with hot and cold running room service over a remote campsite any day—but she prided herself on her ability to build a blazing fire. Dancing flames soon cast a gold glow over the room, making the large space feel cozier and warmer than it actually was.

She pulled nearby giant-sized floor cushions in front of the fire and settled cross-legged on top of them, draping herself with a cashmere blanket taken from the back of one of the leather sofas. She then pushed several marshmallows on a skewer and rotated them over the burning logs, ensuring an even outer brown layer.

A long exhale escaped her. She'd been in what felt like perpetual motion for so long—ever since that summer with Will, in fact. First, accepting Barrett's offer to work for him, climbing steadily from staff assistant to chief of staff thanks to toiling longer and harder than anyone else in his office. Then Barrett had had his first heart attack, prompting him to announce his early retirement from Congress. He'd asked her to prepare Grayson to run for Barrett's seat, ensuring the Monk family political dynasty would continue.

He didn't ask her if she wanted to run.

And she'd done what her stepfather expected of her. She became Grayson's campaign manager, helping him jump to an insurmountable lead in the polls. His election to Congress had been all but assured when he uncovered Barrett's misappropriation of campaign funds, leading Grayson to drop out of the race. After they jointly blew the whistle and Barrett was sentenced to a federal penitentiary, she'd thrown her entire self into planning Grayson's and Nelle's wedding.

It was oddly exhilarating to sit and worry about nothing except the gooeyness of her marshmallows, the melting point of the chocolate and the crunch of the graham crackers.

What did Nelle say when she made the offer to stay at Running Coyote? Staying here would give Finley space and time to figure out what she wanted to do next with her life? That turned out to be the understatement of the century.

If Finley were asked for a list, in order, of her favorite things to do, self-reflection wouldn't make the top ten thousand. She was a doer, not a philosopher. She made things happen.

Well, most things. Will didn't take the offer she made in the paddock. Her stomach panged, and she shoved another marshmallow in her mouth.

But Will was the exception that proved the rule. Normally, she had no trouble coaxing, cajoling and wheedling people into doing her bidding. Not that she exploited her powers for selfish reasons—well, again, except in the case of Will, and he'd had no problem resisting her. But in general, she used them on behalf of others. She pulled off a flawless wedding for Grayson and Nelle. As Barrett's chief of staff, she'd ensured her stepfather faced nothing but smooth sailing.

Of course, Barrett had kept many things from her, not the least of which was his ongoing embezzlement of campaign funds to pay for his lavish lifestyle. Finley had always assumed her stepfather came from inherited wealth—he was the latest in a long line of successful politicians and powerbrokers—but no, his money came from graft and corruption. Which made some of the claims Sadiya reported were in Erica O'Donnell's unpublished book believable. Finley no longer had any doubts that if there was an insider trading ring operating in certain Washington, DC circles, her stepfather would've been in the thick of it.

She sighed. Who was she if she wasn't Barrett's chief of staff? What did she want?

Will's voice asking her the latter question echoed in her head. She took a long swig from the wine bottle, but the burn of the alcohol only intensified the buzzing of his words. Not even the crack and pop of the logs as they broke apart, showers of sparks flying upward, could drown him out.

A shadow moved in the far corner of the room and she jumped. Pinot noir sloshed out of the bottle, dripping onto one of the pillows. "Damn it!"

The shadow grew closer and solidified into Will. He knelt beside her and held out one of her paper napkins. "Here."

She grabbed his offering and dabbed at the spill. The wine had landed on a heavily patterned area and didn't seem to be leaving a noticeable stain. "Heart attack much? You really need to work on announcing your presence."

"Sorry." He settled on the floor next to her. "At least you didn't cut yourself this time."

Whatever calm she had discovered fled at his nearness. Her stomach started to squeeze anew. Maybe s'mores had been a bad idea. "I was just going to bed. I'll leave you here."

But when she moved to stand, Will shook his head. "My room is freezing cold. I'm assuming yours is the same. You did what I was coming out to do—build a fire and sleep in here. Don't be a martyr on my account." He repeated her words back to her with a crooked grin.

"You're not worried I'm going to try to have my way with you?" His rejection still smarted.

He smiled. "Two participated in the kiss. Truce?" Then he nodded at the metal skewers and the bag of marshmallows. "S'mores. Inspired idea."

"Truce." She settled back on her cushion, but every nerve ending thrummed at having him so close. She busied herself by preparing another skewer of marshmallows, giving her hands something to do. "I was tired of peanut butter. And it's only day one."

"With luck, the road will be cleared soon."

"I'd settle for the power being back on." She glanced over at him. "Seriously, what kind of billionaire is your brother-in-law if he can't afford a working generator?"

She was teasing, but Will went still. She frowned.

"He's the kind that gives generously through his foundation. But who doesn't seem to have a lot of time for his new wife," Will eventually said, his gaze distant. Then he shrugged. "Or ranch maintenance. Apparently."

"I'm sorry to hear that. About your sister, I mean." She passed him the skewer and loaded one for herself. They sat, their gazes focused on the toasting marshmallows.

"So am I," said Will into the silence. "I feel responsible since I brought them together. But Lauren insists she's happy."

"Maybe she is." Finley pulled her skewer out of the fire even though the perfect brown had yet to be achieved. Talking about couples who promised each other forever only to discover forever had an expiration date was even further down her list of favorite things to do than self-reflection. "And just because you introduced them, doesn't mean you're responsible."

"Except I am. Reid's company invested in my app. He mentioned being a guinea pig for the initial alpha test, even though the app at the time was mostly populated with friends and family. I thought he was joking but I took him up on his offer anyway. Then he was matched with Lauren. The rest is history."

Finley paused, her s'more halfway to her mouth. "Wait. I'm confused. Your app is some sort of dating service?"

"EverAftr. Yes."

"EverAftr is *you*?" The room spun around Finley. She put her s'more down and grabbed the edges of her cushion, in a vain attempt to anchor herself.

Will ran the hottest matchmaking app in the country? EverAftr's success at generating long-lasting romantic partnerships had received so much publicity that even she, who stayed far away from online dating, had heard of the company.

Will, the man who proved to her that soul mates were mythical, made a fortune off creating pairings filled with hearts and flowers for others?

Yes, the s'mores were definitely a mistake.

"You weren't aware I ran EverAftr?" Will watched her closely. "I don't know if I should be insulted you didn't look me up on the internet. At least occasionally."

"Have you seen how many results are returned when you search 'Will Taylor' on Google?" She swallowed, but it turned into a choke. She started to cough.

"Do you need some water?"

She shook her head, grabbing the bottle of wine and taking a healthy swig instead. "I'm fine," she managed to get out.

"I hope your reaction doesn't mean you had a bad experience with EverAftr."

"No." She gathered her composure as best she could. "Never tried it. Never tried any dating app, for that matter."

"Right. I don't suppose you need help meeting people."

"More like I don't want to." She pressed the back of her hand to her lips. "Sorry. That sounds like I don't enjoy being social. I mean, I don't date."

"That's not the impression I got in the paddock." He took his own swig of pinot noir, but not before she saw his mouth twitch into a smile.

"I'm far from celibate. I just don't…" She shrugged. "Have relationships." She threw him a glance from under her eyelashes. "You missed out. Could have had your mind blown—among other things—with no-strings sex, but you turned me down. Your loss."

"I didn't turn you down, Lee. I said I'm not your toy." He finished off the wine, and then stood. "Want another red? Or should we move to white?"

"Red pairs better with chocolate. Or whiskey," she called after him. Her heart jumped into her throat, beating at least ten thousand times per second. He'd called her Lee. No one called her Lee, except him. And only when he told her he loved her, that long-ago summer.

Will returned with two bottles of red wine held by the neck in his left hand and a decanter of whiskey in his right. He placed them on the tiled hearth, then opened the bottle nearest him and offered it to her. "Want to share or have your own?"

A vision of his mouth on the wine bottle made her shift on her cushion. Sharing was infinitely preferable. "I can't finish a whole one. Surprised you didn't bring glasses, however."

"My hands can only hold so much. Didn't think you'd mind."

She knew exactly how much his hands could hold, and where. "Fine with me. Less to wash."

He chuckled. "Menial labor never was your style."

"I've washed plenty of dishes," she protested. "I clean my own apartment. This isn't the first time you've made a crack about me as if I'm a spoiled princess."

"You grew up among the one percent."

"Excuse me, Mr. EverAftr. Didn't your company

just go public with a capitalization that puts companies like Medevco and HomeHotels to shame? You're one to talk."

"Didn't spend my childhood with a governor of California as a great-grandfather and a congressman for a father."

"Neither did I. Barrett is my stepfather."

"There's a difference?"

Hell, yes. She pressed her lips together tightly and stared into the fire.

Will held out the wine bottle. "Sorry. I'm guessing there was one."

She took it. "I don't mean to reinforce the evil stepparent narrative. Lots of people have caring stepparents who provide them with nothing but love and comfort. And my own father disappeared after I was born and didn't want to have anything to do with me, which makes Barrett parent of the year in comparison." She sighed.

"You never talked much about your family. I didn't know you were related to Barrett until halfway through the internship program."

"For a good reason." She stared into the fire. She told very few people for fear of the rumors of nepotism. She wished she'd never told Will. "I suppose Barrett treated me like he would any daughter. Grayson was a son, and our genders made a difference to him. But Barrett probably shouldn't have been anyone's parent." She grabbed the wine from Will and drank deeply, and then handed it back to him. "Although I think I'm more like Barrett than Grayson ever will be."

"I don't see you going to prison for campaign finance fraud, if that's a consolation."

She laughed. It felt good. She hadn't laughed about Barrett in a very long time. "It is."

The alcohol settled in her stomach, its warm glow traveling along her veins and weighing down her limbs with relaxed languor. At the same time, admitting Barrett had been a less-than-ideal parent made her feel lighter. Younger. More carefree. She no longer had to keep up the pretense of a perfect family for the DC media. Or even for Grayson, who'd bought heavily into the image of his father as a crusading hero until he uncovered Barrett's fraud.

No wonder people said confession was good for the soul.

Of course, she still had to come clean about her own shortcomings. She inhaled, catching Will's gaze with her own, and then blew the breath out. "You weren't wrong, out in the paddock. I was playing a game. I apologize, sincerely. But I never thought of you as a toy. Not earlier today, and not then. You broke my heart, Will."

He blinked, followed by a bark of laughter. "Your heart? You broke mine by breaking up with me. Out of the blue."

"I didn't—"

"You did." All mirth was gone.

"You didn't let me finish. I was going to say I

didn't mean for us to break up." She reached for the bottle, but he kept his grip on it and wouldn't let go.

His gaze, dark and demanding, locked on hers. "Explain."

She gave up on the battle for the wine. She'd just have to get through her confession without an extra shot of liquid courage. "That summer…with the internship ending and graduation approaching, I applied for a position with the State Department."

"I remember. You wanted to travel."

"Yep." And she never did. Not as she intended. "But what I didn't tell you is Barrett called me into his office shortly before I had my interview. Said he received reports I was… I believe the word *gallivanting* was used…with another intern."

"Most college-aged people gallivant. In one form or another."

"Ah, but they weren't Barrett Monk's stepdaughter. A reflection on his distinguished family and storied name. And you have to admit, we gallivanted quite a lot. And weren't very discreet." She nodded at the bottle still held tightly in his hands. "Seriously, I could use some of that."

Will shook his head. "I want to know this is you talking and not the alcohol."

"Fine." She hugged her knees to her chest. "Barrett threatened to torpedo my application. Said I wasn't appropriately respectful of the opportunities he was providing. I needed to prove to him I was worthy of being a member of the Monk family. Which meant cutting out all extraneous activities. Like you."

Will's gaze burned into her. "Why didn't you say anything? I would have understood."

Hindsight being 20/20, of course she should've told Will everything. Been honest and up-front. Laid everything on the table. But she'd been twenty-one years old, an adult but not a worldly one, painfully young in so many ways. And above all, anxious for Barrett's approval.

She never knew her biological father, who'd left when she was an infant. Her mother had married Barrett shortly after, but after a long illness had passed away when Finley was thirteen. Barrett had become the only parent she had. And like most children, she'd wanted to make her parent proud—especially because Barrett rarely showed any form of affection, causing her to chase his approval even harder.

It had taken much mental health counseling over the past year to recognize the harmful patterns in her family relationships. But her realizations couldn't change the past. "I thought Barrett was right," she said finally. "He knew Washington. He understood politics. He had knowledge and experience on his side."

Will shook his head. "I get that. I don't get why you didn't tell me."

She saw the decanter out of the corner of her eye and grabbed it, removing the top to take a stiff drink. Whiskey fumes stung her nose as the liquid scorched her throat. She welcomed the momentary pain. "I stupidly thought if you and I were 'soul mates'—" she rolled her eyes "—as you insisted we were, then we'd stay together. Surely, nothing could separate us for good. Not even if I told you we should break up. You would just…dismiss…that hurdle."

She scoffed at her naivety, expecting Will to join in. But he stayed silent and still. So still, she was tempted to check if he continued to breathe. "You were very convincing," he finally said.

A log popped in the fireplace. The fire had dwindled to a few lone flames among the embers. She couldn't see his expression very well. But she was fairly certain the tightness in her throat was matched by his.

"Barrett persuaded me I needed to be. He said…" She reached again for the whiskey. "He said you were using me. For my connections and family name. For access to him." Will's left hand made a sudden movement. She hastened to add, "I assured him otherwise."

"I don't understand," Will repeated. "Why did you listen to him?"

Why? It was a question she'd asked herself more times than she cared to admit. "He was so adamant, so sure he was right. And—" She squeezed her eyes shut. "You have to admit using people to get ahead was an everyday occurrence in DC. I was scared. Maybe he was right. Maybe you didn't love me as much as I loved you. Maybe I was a stepping-stone to be discarded."

"How could you think that? No. Strike that. How could you think *I* thought that? I loved you. You knew that." His voice was a harsh whisper in the darkness.

"I thought I did." Her stomach flip-flopped at the

past tense and she took another sip. The whiskey didn't wash away the acrid taste the memory left in her mouth. "You need to know, Barrett showed me the letters."

"What letters?"

"C'mon, Will. The recommendations he wrote on your behalf for Harvard, Yale and Stanford Law. I don't blame you, I knew you wanted to be a lawyer, to right great wrongs—"

"I never—" Will exploded. "I didn't—that's a lie. I never received recommendations from him."

"I saw them."

"Doesn't mean I asked for the letters. Or even wanted him to write ones for me." He jerked a hand through his hair. "Damn it, Finley. You should have said something."

She hugged her knees tighter, her head falling to rest on them. She could see so clearly now what she'd been blind to for most of her entire life. Of course Barrett had faked the recommendations, just like he and his campaign treasurer had faked the finance records sent to the Federal Election Commission. She, who prided herself on always being ten steps in front of others, had let Barrett string her along like a child's pull toy for years. Will was only confirming her worst suspicions. "I know that. Now."

Will exhaled, harsh and sharp. "I never went to law school."

She turned her head toward him. "What? That was all you talked about. I made sure Barrett sent the recommendations, despite our break-up. Why didn't you go?"

He made an impatient movement. "I—why didn't you join the State Department?"

"They turned me down." The memory still hurt, although it wasn't nearly as painful as the thoughts of Will over the years. "Barrett then offered me a role in his office. I stayed and worked my way up—and I earned those promotions by being very good at what I do. Why didn't you study law?"

He opened his mouth, then shut it and shrugged instead. "Things turned out okay."

"CEO of EverAftr? Yes. I'd say so." She tried for a smile, his refusal to answer her questions about law school cutting a little closer to the bone than she liked. "Surprised you named the app that. Since 'happily-ever-after' is nothing but a cute fairy tale for little children and the giant media companies after their parents' money."

"You don't believe that."

"You can't possibly believe otherwise. You're too smart."

Will's unreadable gaze searched hers. Then he turned his head to stare into dying flames. "The name tested well. Marketing liked it."

With a start, she realized she hadn't expected him to agree with her. She wanted him to argue with her, to persuade her she was wrong. The fact that he didn't…

Well. Enough strolling down memory lane. Confession might be beneficial for her soul, but it was hell on her equanimity. She should return to her room. Her cold room. Alone.

She put the top back on the whiskey decanter and stood up. "This is where I say good night."

"Lee."

She froze, resolving to see a cardiologist when the road opened. Her continual rapid pulse couldn't be good for her health. "Yes?"

"I don't remember you believing 'happily-ever-after' was a myth."

The room was wreathed in heavy shadows. Hopefully, he couldn't see her face. Couldn't discern her naked yearning to turn back the clock fifteen years and tell Barrett where to shove his fake letters of recommendation. Wouldn't perceive just how much she regretted not having stronger faith in him, in their love.

But the past could not be rewritten. "I once bought into it," she said. "But I grew up."

He rose to his feet and stood next to her. So close, the tiny hairs on her arms vibrated with awareness. "I'm sorry," he said.

She creased her forehead. "For what? The breakup was my doing. This morning was my doing. I owe you more apologies than there were raindrops in last night's storm."

"For not convincing you I loved you for you."

An unfamiliar prickling sensation came from her nose. "You were convincing. I chose not to trust the evidence. But thank you for the thought." On impulse, scarcely knowing what she was doing before she did it, she leaned up to kiss his stubbled cheek.

He turned his head at the last second. Her mouth landed on his.

Sparks ignited, setting her veins on fire. She opened her mouth, her tongue imploring his lips to open, plunging inside when he acquiesced to her demand. His tongue met hers, an intense dance of heat and pressure, and she was lost to the unique magic that was kissing Will. Her arms twined around his neck, her chest pressing into his as she tried to burrow closer, pull herself deeper into him.

A log fell in the fireplace with a loud crash. They broke apart at the sound. Finley looked up at Will from under her lashes. "Sorry, I didn't mean to break the truce."

"Don't apologize." Will's gaze reflected the flames dancing in the fireplace. His hands tightened on her waist. "I was a willing participant."

She licked her lips. They were swollen. She could still taste Will. "But you said in the paddock—"

"I'll repeat what I asked this morning. Is this what you really want or is it another game?"

She was about to faint from want. Her knees were soft with it. Her arms ached. Her sex throbbed, demanding more. Demanding him. "We're not meant for happily-ever-after. But for tonight, I want this. I want you."

"Tonight." His mouth closed over hers.

Ten

Will kissed Finley, storing up memories like so many precious gems. His near-perfect recall meant he would always remember this night, even as part of him still questioned if Finley was actually in his arms, her mouth hot on his, or it was a very vivid dream.

But nothing in his dreams ever approached the marvel that was kissing Finley now. They'd been relatively inexperienced kids that summer, not virgins, but still learning how to give and receive pleasure from a partner. Now, Finley's knowing lips and tongue gave as good as he gave. Desire ignited into an inferno, so hot, so fast, he didn't know if his senses would ever fully recover.

He trailed openmouthed kisses down her neck,

over to her ear, wondering if her skin behind her ear was still sensitive. He licked and then ran his teeth lightly over the area. She gasped and shivered, pressing her belly hard against him.

He took that as a yes.

Her loose T-shirt was in his way. He bunched it up, running his hands over the curve of her abdomen, the indentation of her waist. It turned out his memory wasn't nearly perfect after all, for he'd forgotten how her skin glowed like luminescent silk, the way she shuddered when his fingers traced patterns up and down her spine.

She stepped back and pulled her T-shirt all the way off, revealing her breasts. His breath stuttered. Finley at twenty-one had been stunning. Finley now was…magnificent. Confident and aware of her power, a goddess by any measure. She knelt on the cushions in front of the fire, her gaze dark with invitation.

He didn't need to be asked twice. She leaned in to kiss him, placing his hands on her breasts, their weight and shape at once familiar but new. He set to learning them again, his fingers teasing one perfect globe then the other, pulling and rolling the tight, hard peaks the way she had once taught him to do. She collapsed against him, her breath coming fast and harsh.

Then she pushed him back, tugging his T-shirt over his head. Her thumbs brushed over his abs with feather-light strokes, dipping below the waistband of his sweatpants, lingering near but never quite touching his impossibly hard cock. He gritted his teeth, sweating with impatience, wanting her hand on him, her mouth, to bury himself deep and lose himself inside her, now. But also wanting this night to last forever.

How was this possible? After all these years, after numerous sexual encounters, and several girlfriends later—some of whom he cared for considerably—and he was about to come from just knowing the person touching him was Finley.

With supreme effort, he removed her hand and tugged her to lie down beside him. Her yoga pants were an unnecessary barrier and he made quick work of discarding them, baring the dark triangle at the apex of her thighs. She sighed, her legs opening for him, her arms reaching. But he was a firm believer that turnabout equaled fair play. Keeping a tight grip on his self-control, he drew decreasing concentric circles from her rounded belly to the tops of her thighs, his fingers coming ever closer but never arriving at the tangled nest of curls. She writhed, her hips jerking, seeking.

"I concede," she panted, and rolled them both until he was on his back and she was looking down at him, black wings of hair falling to frame her face.

He'd never seen anyone more beautiful.

"Condom?" she asked.

The air escaped him. "In my bag. In my room."

She smiled, slow and sinful and full of promise. "Then we'll just have to improvise. I'm not letting you leave only to change your mind."

"Not going to happen."

"I know." She kissed him, her tongue lapping at

his. Then she kissed her way down his throat, to his sternum, taking her time to lavish his nipples with wet, hot attention before raising her head to whisper in his ear. "Because I'm finally going to turn my favorite fantasy into reality."

Her hand grasped him then. Her fingers already knew how he liked to be stroked, what pressure to apply and where. His brain threatened to shut down. Her touch was too much for his nerve endings. She was too much. She watched him for a minute, her smile a mix of delight and sin, her hooded gaze shining. Then she lowered her head and took him in her clever, knowing mouth.

He wasn't going to last longer than zero point one three seconds. That wouldn't do.

He sat up, taking her off guard. Then he tugged her down on the cushions until it was her turn to blink up at him. "Was I doing something wrong?" she asked.

"No. Too much too right," he growled. Then he pulled her legs apart and buried his mouth in her wet heat, seeking her most sensitive spots. She screamed, a chorus of angels to his ears. He loved making Finley scream. He loved that he could still make her scream.

Her back arched. He held her steady, letting her know he had her, that it was safe to let go. He fell automatically into the rhythm he knew she liked best, using his tongue and fingers to coax and push and demand, until she broke and shattered in his grasp. His name was a chant on her lips.

Nothing, not even all the success of EverAftr, gave him the same sense of satisfaction as knowing he caused Finley Smythe to fall apart. He held her as she quieted, pulling the blanket she'd discarded earlier over them. Her chest rose and fell against him, her mouth lax against the side of his neck.

Her fingers enlaced with his.

His heart twisted. Out of everything they had just experienced, holding her hand felt the most intimate of all. Like she belonged there, by his side. Giving her strength to him, taking his strength for herself.

For tonight.

Morning sun teased Will's eyelids. He turned his head away from the source of light, resisting the temptation to open his eyes. What if last night really had been a dream? What if he woke up and Finley wasn't next to him?

They'd retired to his room, although not much sleep had been achieved. He should be bone-tired but exhilaration powered his nervous system. He hadn't felt this good upon awaking since…okay, fine. Since he and Finley had first slept together, all those years ago.

He reached out his hand, seeking the warm satin of Finley's skin. He encountered nothing but rumpled sheets. His eyes flew open.

Last night had been real. Her scent lingered, pomegranate and spice and sugar. The pillow next to his bore the imprint of her head. His body would forever be branded by her touch.

But where was she? He sat up, throwing back the

covers that had cocooned them, and swung his legs out of bed. His sweatpants were…somewhere.

Finley laughed from the doorway. His heart clenched at the sight of her. She was fully dressed, wearing a fresh pair of jeans that clung to her hips and thighs and a blue flannel shirt that matched the sky outside the window. In her hands she carried a plate of what looked like peanut butter sandwiches. "I was hoping to serve you breakfast in bed, but you seem to be getting out of it."

He settled back on his pillow. "Serve away."

She sat on the edge of the bed next to him and handed him a sandwich. "Sorry for the monotonous menu. But surprise! I found a manual can opener. Canned salmon for lunch. Yum. Y'know, we should decide when we think the refrigerator is a lost cause and rescue some of the cheese before everything spoils. Knowing Nelle, I'm sure she requested some fancy, gourmet varieties to be stocked."

Finley was babbling. She only babbled when she wanted to divert someone—in this case, him—from having a serious conversation. He set the sandwich aside and tried to catch her gaze. "You're up early."

"Horses wait for no man. Or for any gender." She played with her sandwich but didn't take a bite. "You'll be happy to know both Trudy and Ranger have been fed and watered. In fact, I was thinking I might go for a ride. A horseback ride," she clarified with her familiar smirk. "Want to join me? Trudy is very sweet. I can teach you the basics, if you want."

If she thought they were going to turn the clock

back to wary acquaintances sharing a house because they had no other choice, she was mistaken. Not after last night. "Tell me what's really going on inside your head, Lee."

She inhaled sharply. "You should know that I'm not fond of nicknames."

"Yes, you are."

"Yes, I *was*." She stressed the last word. Then she indicated the view from the window. "What's going on inside my head? I want to go riding. It's glorious outside. You should get up and see for yourself. California is spectacular after a winter rainstorm. The mountains are sharp and clear against the sky. The air is crisp—"

"Your head is going in circles about last night."

She raised her eyebrows in polite inquiry. "Oh? It is? You're that familiar with the contents of my head?"

"You're obsessing over what happened between us and if there will be a repeat. As I am. And I think there should be a repeat. As often as possible. If you want, of course."

She blinked at him, shock and not a little yearning written on her face. Then she turned away, her gaze focusing anywhere but on him. "Look, I know our situation must reek to you of a storybook. Two former lovers trapped together, old misunderstandings are discussed, dormant feelings combust, yadda yadda yadda, blah blah blah. But I don't do relationships. I don't do happily-ever-afters. And that's what your company sells. I don't blame you for internalizing your own marketing."

He held up his hands. "Whoa. Who said anything about a happily-ever-after?" Although, if he were honest with himself, the idea was more than a tickle in the back of his mind. "You're the one who mentioned mind-blowing, no-strings-attached sex. Can't fault a guy for being intrigued."

"Did you think that was what I was offering last night?" Her brows drew together, for a split second only, before her expression smoothed out. Then her slow smile reappeared. "Good. As long as we're on the same page." She held out her right hand. "I propose new truce terms. No-strings-sex until one of us is bored?"

He answered her by pulling her head to his, taking her mouth, demanding she open to him. She sighed and relaxed into him, her arms wrapping around his neck, her tongue seeking his. Something crashed to the floor. He didn't care. He had Finley back, and he wasn't going to let her use her words to create barriers between them again.

"The sandwiches—" she gasped.

"Only hungry for you." Her Western-style shirt was fastened with snaps instead of buttons, making it easy to rip open. Her breasts were encased in scraps of lace that enhanced rather than hid their perfection. He played with a tightly furled nipple, rolling it with his fingers, brushing the tip with his thumb, before leaning down to draw the sweet bud, lace and all, into his mouth. His cock throbbed but he ignored his insistent need. The more he kept Finley drunk on desire, the less time for her to come up with reasons to put distance between them.

Her hands came up to his chest, but she used them to push him away, insistent enough that he drew back. He shrugged off the disappointment threatening to crush him. "No?"

She shook her head. "Hell, yes. But fast. Hard. Now." She shimmied out of her jeans, revealing another scrap of lace just barely covering her mound. But before he could drink his fill of the tantalizing sight, her mouth was on him, pulling on his aching length, begging his full attention. He swelled to improbable dimensions in her warm, perceptive mouth, tormenting his most sensitive zones with pleasure so intense, he wasn't sure he would survive an orgasm.

Where was his recall of baseball statistics when he needed them for a distraction? He couldn't think. His neurons were replaced by nerve endings that could only feel. "Lee," he gasped. "Stop. Or slow down."

"If you say so." She released him with a smile, her cheeks flushed bright red, her breasts rapidly rising and falling. Last night, he'd thought Finley in the firelight was stunning beyond belief. But that vision didn't compare to Finley in the sunlight, kneeling on the bed, her gaze wide and wild. His chest constricted at her beauty. "But be careful what you wish for," she breathed.

She reached for a foil packet on his bedside table, one of the few remaining after last night. Without taking her gaze away from his, she rolled the condom onto his cock. Then she brushed the scrap of lace aside and guided him inside her.

His eyes nearly rotated to the back of his head. Then she bore down, burying his length even deeper in her wet, hot sex, and he was lost. The primal rhythm they generated together took over, as they moved in tandem faster, building the pressure higher. He circled his thumb around the sensitive cluster of nerves at her entrance and she screamed, shuddering as she bore down on him, demanding he not stay behind.

He let go and flew with her.

Finley collapsed on top of him and he cradled her close, smiling when her rapid breaths calmed into light snuffling snores. Languor weighted his limbs, but he fought the urge to drift into unconsciousness with her.

Pieces of the puzzle that had tormented him for years suddenly fell into place. They'd been young. Perhaps if they had met in their late twenties or thirties, they would have had enough perspective to weather interference by others. But they had been punch-drunk on love and each other, and neither had the worldly experience nor self-confidence to ask questions when the relationship went off the rails.

He didn't blame Finley, not now. Yes, she should have been honest with him. But he'd had his own run-in with Barrett—not over letters of recommendation, that was a damn lie—but they'd bumped into each other in the hallways of the Capitol. When Will eagerly introduced himself to the congressman, Barrett had given him a thorough once-over and silently put Will in his place, ignoring Will's proffered hand. Then Barrett had stepped past him and started a collegial conversation with Will's co-intern, the son of a Dartmouth dean.

The implication Will wasn't important enough to acknowledge, even with a handshake, still rankled. He hadn't told Finley after it happened because he didn't want to open up the possibility she would defend her stepfather. But he'd seen for himself the force of Barrett's personality. It would not have been easy for a young Finley to tell him no.

The more Will thought about Finley's words of the night before, the more he realized Barrett had manipulated them both. He'd played on Finley's fear of not being loved for herself. And he'd used Will's insecurity, that of a working class kid struggling to keep up with those born with the proverbial silver spoon in their mouths, to do so. Will would lay a hefty bet the only reason Finley didn't get the State Department position was because Barrett torpedoed her chances so she would come work for him.

But that was then. Now, there was no way Will would let another fifteen years go by without her in his life, much less fifteen minutes. And it wasn't just the sex, as astonishing as they were together. He'd missed *her*. Her intelligence, her snark, her charm— even when she'd tried to manipulate him.

She might want to think there weren't any strings attached, but he intended to fasten them securely before they left the ranch.

Finley snuggled closer, her legs entwining with his in her sleep. He yawned, reveling in the soft, warm weight of her. Maybe a nap wasn't such a bad idea…

His eyes flew open. He had a contract to star in a reality television series. Screenweb had already sent him their advertising concepts, built around the CEO of EverAftr using his own app to find a perfect match. But how could he search for a partner who fulfilled his ideal criteria when his perfectly imperfect match was in his arms?

Eleven

Finley walked into the ranch's main room, dressed for her morning horseback ride. In the last three days, she and Will had fallen into a routine: breakfast together, then Finley fed the horses before taking one of them out on the trails dotting the hills around the ranch. Will stayed behind, working on ideas for Ever-Aftr until she returned to the house, then they foraged in the kitchen to make lunch. The rest of the hours were spent talking and making love until the sun threatened to make its appearance.

They had a lot of conversations to catch up on.

Will was already hard at work. He sat on one of the leather couches in front of the fireplace, scrawling intently on a yellow legal pad. She took a seat next to him and dropped a kiss on his cheek. "It's

Trudy's turn to be ridden today, so I might be back a little later than usual. She likes to ramble."

Will frowned, still focused on what he was writing. "Be safe out there."

"Trudy knows this area like the back of her hoof. We'll be fine." She looked down at his pad. It consisted mostly of scratched-out words. "Doesn't look like you're making lots of progress on whatever you're doing."

He glanced up. "What?"

She pointed to his scribblings. "You've crossed everything out."

"Oh." He looked back at it. "Brainstorming. Not enough brain, too little storm."

She laughed. "You have a very big brain and as for storms…" She pulled his head to hers and kissed him until they were both breathless, the heat on constant simmer between them flaring into a supernova. "I see lightning, multiple times a night."

"Just at night?" he joked, rubbing his thumb over her lower lip.

"Don't push your luck. I've already complimented you." She smiled and kissed him again before sitting back. "What are you brainstorming? Maybe I can help. The horses can wait a few minutes."

"What do you know about television production? Specifically, reality TV."

She shook her head. "Not my area of expertise, unless we're talking media appearances on news channels."

His lips thinned, and he added to the scribbles on his page. "Right. The media. Forgot about them."

She narrowed her gaze. "Wait. You don't like movies—"

"I like them. I don't have the time—"

She waved his protest away. "So why are you asking about television production? TV is nothing but a string of mini-movies, even reality series. And if you don't have two hours for a film, you're not going to have ten or twenty-two hours."

"I do if the series is based on EverAftr."

She leaned back on the sofa. "Oh. Wow."

"The meeting in LA I missed thanks to the mudslide? It was with the streaming service that commissioned the series. To kick off the production."

"Is that what you're brainstorming? Ideas for episodes?"

"In a way." His lips pressed into a thin line.

"Let me see what you have—" She reached for the legal pad but he put it down out of her reach and turned on the sofa to face her.

"I have a better idea. Let's go on a date. A real date. Tonight."

If he was seeking a diversion, it worked. "A date? Tonight?" She laughed. "And go where? I think we've explored the house pretty thoroughly. Even the pool." The memory of just how they'd occupied themselves in the water caused a rush of heat to her cheeks. Who needed a working pool heater with Will around?

"Let me worry about that." He indicated the pad.

"I need to work most of today. Pick you up outside your room at six?"

"You're aware I'm already sleeping with you, right? You don't need to woo me."

He raised his eyebrows. "Don't I?"

His question made her stomach flop, half queasy, half thrilled by a hope she dared not examine. She leaned up and kissed him lightly on the cheek. "You're being ridiculous, but I accept. See you at six."

"Wear something nice," he called after her.

She shook her head, laughing as she exited the room. Yes, he was ridiculous. But he was her type of ridiculous.

Giving him up when the time came was going to be difficult, but she'd manage.

By six o'clock, Finley's fluttering nerves had expanded from her stomach to her chest and down to her knees. Not even a galloping run on Trudy followed by a cold shower could calm down the roiling mixture of anticipation, dread, desire and pessimistic optimism that currently accompanied her every thought. Still, she dressed herself carefully for her "date," digging into her suitcase to find the dress she'd brought as a backup for Nelle and Grayson's rehearsal dinner. The long gown had been a gift from Nelle, an ephemeral blush pink concoction of silk and organza. It wasn't Finley's usual style, but Nelle had explained it reminded her of what a fairy godmother might wear— not the frumpy fairy godmothers seen in animated films, but the kind who made the impossible happen, like helping Nelle and Grayson find their way back to each other.

Finley had to admit the dress flattered her. She rarely wore pink as it tended to wash her out, but in the candlelight this shade made appear radiant. The neckline dipped low over her breasts, the fabric skimming her curves until the skirt flared out into layers of organza below her hips. She twirled in front of the mirror, and then laughed at herself. She was as nervous as she'd been as a twenty-one-year-old, waiting for Will to pick her up for the first time.

A knock sounded. She blew out the candles with some difficulty, her breathing already affected by anticipation of the night to come, and opened the door to reveal Will. He was hopelessly attractive in a dark blue suit that matched his eyes. In his hands he held a small bouquet of purple and gold pansies. "Only flower I could find in the gardens."

Her heart twinged. The date had just started and already he was finding chinks in her determination to resist any sentiment. "Thank you."

He offered her his left arm. "Shall we?"

She couldn't help her wide grin. "Of course. Lead on."

As they walked in silence through the now-familiar corridors, her fingers gripped the fine wool of his jacket. When they passed the living area, she looked up at him with surprise. "Will?"

"Almost there."

He led her out a side door she'd never used, and down a winding stone pathway. At the bottom of the slope, a one-story stucco cottage that matched the ranch house's architecture came into view. She stopped. "On the ranch map, isn't this marked as a private office?"

He smiled. "Reid had it built for Lauren. Off-limits to guests."

"Then maybe we shouldn't go inside."

Will nuzzled her cheek. "I'm not a guest."

He guided her to the cottage's front door, and then opened the wood and iron door with a flourished bow. "Welcome."

"Oh…my…" Finley stood transfixed on the doorstep.

The door opened into a large room that occupied the entire footprint of the cottage. The walls were lined with mahogany bookcases that soared from the terra-cotta-tiled floor to the high ceiling far above. At the far end, a spiral staircase provided access to a loft heaped with pillows. Lit candles were everywhere, their flickering light turning the space into an enchanted wonderland.

"I feel like I'm in *Beauty and the Beast*," she murmured. "All that's missing is a talking teapot."

Will glanced at her. "I don't remember a talking teapot in the fairy tale."

She blinked. "I'm referring to the film—or rather, two films. And a Broadway musical. You know what, never mind." She walked into the room, her gaze struggling to take everything in and store the details. "This is…stunning."

Will smiled. "I thought you might like it."

She gave him a mock glare. "I can't believe you held this out on me."

"Where do you think I was, that first day after we argued in the paddock? I came here to work." He took her hand and guided her to the middle of the room, where a small round table had been set with paper plates containing sandwiches. "If I'd been in the house, I would've finished what we started."

"I was too ashamed of my behavior to come out of my room. Now I wish I'd have looked for you. But if I'd found you in here, believe me, sex would have been the last thing on my mind." Her head was on a constant swivel, as she took in as many details as she could: the overstuffed wing-backed chairs upholstered in jewel tones. The massive oak desk in its own alcove. The stained glass windows reflecting the candlelight.

"In that case, we're going back to the house. Now."

"Oh no, we're not. When will I ever get the chance to dine in a place like this?" She leaned up and kissed him on the cheek. "Thank you. Even if the main course is rather familiar."

He handed her a glass of red wine. "But we have a damn good bottle of Margaux, thanks to Reid's wine cellar." He picked up his own glass and clinked it against hers. "Cheers. Here's to our second first date."

She sipped her wine, still taking in her surroundings. Or maybe looking around gave her an excuse to avoid the emotions shining in Will's gaze. Emotions she didn't dare name. Naming them would make the feelings real.

"I can't believe how many books are in here."

"Lauren has collected books all her life. Reid built this to store her library."

"But I thought the ranch wasn't their primary residence?"

"It's not. Which means Lauren rarely sees her collection." Will drank deeply from his glass. "May I interest you in an appetizer of canned pears?"

The table he'd set looked tiny to her eyes. They would be sitting very close together. Intimate. Her heart knocked hard against her ribs.

Silly to fear intimacy when she and Will were still clothed and vertical, especially since they barely kept their hands off each other over the past few days. But Finley was very careful not to confuse sex with love.

She enjoyed sex. It felt good, in much the same way a satisfying scratch of an itch did. She had fun and her partners did, too. But physical sensations were one thing. Emotions were quite another.

Tonight's dinner with Will loomed like an invisible line in the sand. If she stepped over it, she feared she would no longer be able to pretend there was nothing between them but a chemical reaction. Although, if she were honest, she'd admit she left that line far behind the night they spent in front of the fire.

"Do you mind if I explore more first?" She walked to the bookcase on the opposite wall, next to the alcove that held the desk. Putting as much space as she could place between them.

Above her head, first editions of Nancy Drew mysteries published over the decades occupied an entire shelf. To her left, she found a large section devoted to West African literature, and below that, histories of various Latin American countries written in Spanish. "I think I'd like your sister. What caused her to start collecting books?"

Will joined her. But his gaze wasn't on the shelves. He regarded her with longing and... Her cheeks filled with heat. "I'd rather discuss other topics than my sister," he rumbled. "Like us. What we're doing. And what happens after we leave the ranch."

Finley's pulse whooshed in her ears. She knew what would happen when they left the ranch. They would part. She would return to her messy, snarled life. Will would go back to earning accolades for running his successful company. That was the only possible outcome.

"I have a better idea." She leaned into him, nuzzling the side of his neck. "Let's forget the appetizer and go straight to the main course."

"You're that hungry for peanut butter?"

"No." She kissed him, her tongue seeking and finding his, igniting the spark that was never fully dormant between them.

He kissed her back, but when her hands ventured lower, he broke off the contact and stepped back. "Don't get me wrong. I like this. A lot. But I was hoping for a more traditional date. The kind where we talk first."

"Since when were we ever traditional?" She closed the distance he put between them. The silk of her dress did nothing to conceal her nipples, hard with need. And she wasn't the only one. The front of his trousers bore ample evidence.

"Lee—" he started, then stopped with a groan when her hands found what they had sought, stroking him through the fine wool.

"You're hungry, too," she whispered in his ear. "Don't deny it."

"I could never deny you. But—"

Through her peripheral vision, she spotted the desk. She hopped up on its broad surface. The flimsy organza of her skirt rode up. His gaze zeroed in on her bared thighs.

He always did have a thing for her legs.

"But what?" She made herself comfortable on the edge of the desk, leaning back on her elbows. If her skirt bunched even higher, revealing to Will she wore only the barest scraps of lace underneath the dress, that might have been on purpose.

"My laptop is behind you. Pretty much a dead paperweight now, but maybe we should…"

She glanced over her shoulder and then laughed. "Sorry, I didn't see it. You're right. Breaking your computer would be a mood killer." She slid off the desk and whispered in Will's ear. "But breaking the desk? I look forward to it."

She picked up the open laptop and handed it to Will, grabbing the file folder that was underneath. A printout fluttered to the ground. She bent down.

The hot glow winked out of Will's gaze. "I'll take that."

"Your hands are full—hey." She stood, examining

the piece of paper in her hand. "This is a draft press release for your TV show. How exciting." She grinned at him before starting to read out loud. "*Finding Ever-Aftr* is a reality television series where real-life singles use the highly successful EverAftr dating app to find a life partner perfectly matched to their personal strengths, weaknesses and desired attributes—"

"Lee. Stop. Let's have dinner. We need to talk—"

She waved him off. "The company's CEO, William Taylor—" she smiled at him "—is the star of the first season of eight one-hour episodes as he sets out on his own quest for his own happily-ever-after..."

She blinked. Hard. Then she blinked again. The text on the page remained blurry. Whoever printed the press release out needed to change the ink cartridge, because the rest of it was illegible. She took a shuddering breath, and the words swam into sharper focus. "... He'll be joined by six other people from across the United States, of all ages and from all walks of life, with only one question in common—can the world's most popular dating app really lead to *Finding EverAftr*?"

The room tilted on an axis before righting itself. Her hands were so numb, she almost dropped the printout. But her years of political training rescued her. She dredged up a bright smile and pasted it on her face. "Well," she said, affecting an airy shrug, "for the topic of your next brainstorm, I suggest finding a better writer for your press releases. I can recommend excellent PR agencies, but they're mostly based in DC. But I'm sure if you ask them for references—"

"This is why I wanted to have dinner. To tell you about the series." His hands clenched and unclenched by his sides. "And to tell you I've already sent word to the production company via Tim. I'm not going to be in it."

She laughed, a little too loud. "Why not? I might criticize the press release's style, but the content is fab. A tech CEO using his own service on camera for all to judge? It's a brilliant concept. People will be on the edges of their seats to see if EverAftr works for the man who came up with it." She stretched her grin farther. "Congrats. This is terrific stuff."

He grabbed the press release from her, crumbling it into a ball. "Yes, this is good exposure for the company. Otherwise, we wouldn't have agreed." He tossed the ball across the room. Turning back to her, he cupped her face with his hands. "But as for being in it… How can I, after the last few days?"

"Will." The floor threatened to fall from under her feet. Her vision blurred again, and blinking didn't clear it. "The last few days have been…" Now her voice was cracking. "They've been the stuff of fantasies. Believe me, I will make productive use of the memories when I'm alone. But we have a no-strings agreement—"

He kissed her. A gentle kiss, promising an unspoken future. A promise she knew he would not keep. Not because he didn't want to, but because she knew it just wasn't possible. "We did have one. But this is a date. You agreed to it."

She searched his gaze. For a brief second, she lost

herself in his gray-blue depths, allowing herself to believe that they could be more, that they could leave the ranch and build a relationship despite any hurdles in their way. But even as she let herself imagine Will might be right, she knew it was illusory. She'd had a lifetime of experiences that proved love didn't conquer anything. Her mother had loved her father, but he'd abandoned her with an infant to take care of. Barrett had demonstrated over and over to her that relationships were transactional, nothing more. And yes, Finley had forced the fight with Will that led to their breakup, but they weren't confident enough in their feelings for each other to weather the first big storm that came along.

Once the road off the ranch opened, any possible future they had together would slam closed.

But in the meantime, they were still stuck on the ranch thanks to a literal storm. No need to ruin the time they still had together. What was the harm in humoring his fantasy? She was indulging in several of her own, after all. Fantasies like becoming accustomed to waking up next to someone she adored. Or having breakfast with someone who made her laugh just as easily as making her sigh with desire as a matter of course.

He'd come to his senses as soon as they joined the real world again. They both would.

"Okay." She smiled at him. "This is a date, so let's have dinner like you planned. And you can talk. I promise to listen."

He escorted her to the table, poured her another

glass of wine and launched into the history of how he was approached to be on the series. She even laughed at some of his stories. But as Finley looked around the library, she decided it was just a room. A very pretty, delightful room, but it wasn't enchanted. And they may be currently trapped by forces out of their control, but she was not a princess. There wouldn't be a happily-ever-after for her once they were allowed to leave.

Twelve

Finley returned from her ride sore and exhausted, but from wrangling her thoughts instead of wrangling the horse.

The date last night had been a success…somewhat. Despite eventually finishing what they started on the library's desk and then retiring to Will's room for even more earth-shattering activities, she'd been unable to sleep. She'd slipped out of his bed earlier than normal and saddled Ranger, hoping a long gallop would help her sort through the thoughts bouncing around like multiple pinballs. Instead, the conflicting feelings warring for primacy only intensified, the pressure in her brain building to almost migraine levels, and her headache was not helped when she realized she'd let Ranger travel farther afield than she intended. By the time she pulled open the French doors that led to the breakfast room off the kitchen, she was ready for lunch and a quick shower—and only wished she could do both at the same time. "Will?"

He didn't answer her call. But there was something different about the house. The atmosphere seemed brighter, louder. There was a faint humming noise that hadn't been there before... And was that Will's voice? Was he talking to Tim on the CB radio? She followed the sound into the kitchen and froze with shock.

Appliances blinked blue and red lights. The ice-making machine in the refrigerator clanked. Copper and glass pendant lamps shone down from above.

The power had been restored to the ranch.

Will wasn't on the radio. He was on his cell phone. He caught her eye and gave her a smile and a thumbs-up, indicating the clock flashing "12:00" on the microwave. But she couldn't help but notice the deep furrows now creasing his forehead as he returned to his call. She acknowledged him with a wave, then ran/walked to the guest suite where she still kept most of her things. Her phone. She needed her phone.

She flew to the bedside table where she'd plugged her phone into the charger, just in case. The screen lit up. If she were prone to crying, she might have wept at the sight. She did do a little jig in place.

So many possibilities to choose from! She could read her email. She could go on the internet. She could call Sadiya—oh.

Her exultation fled.

She'd always been keenly aware their time at the ranch had an expiration date. The power company would restore electricity, the crews would clear the road and the bubble that had contained them would pop.

But now that the bubble had been breached, she realized she'd avoided planning her next steps. After all, the longer they stayed isolated on the ranch, the better for her. The claims in Erica O'Donnell's book would stay far away. She could ignore the ugly mess that was the remnants of a career she once loved.

She could let herself daydream about taking Will up on the future she saw shining in his gaze.

During her ride, she'd realized she was being selfish. He had a life, too. A life that wasn't knotted up with salacious rumors and tawdry scandals. A life of purpose, with people who depended on him. A life that deserved a partner who matched his strengths and complemented his weaknesses.

The life he was headed toward before a winter storm stranded him with her.

She unlocked her phone. The screen came alive with alerts for texts, missed calls and news articles. She was about to swipe and dismiss them in favor of calling Sadiya, but the top news alert caught her eye.

"Bombshell book from senator's wife promises dirt on insider trading, sex scandal."

She sank onto the bed. Erica O'Donnell's memoirs were no longer under wraps.

Sadiya answered on the first ring. "There you are! Are you back in civilization?"

"No. Road is still blocked. I checked on it while out for a horseback ride this morning. But the power is finally back, so I have a working phone."

"Great. Because we need to talk and I didn't want to leave this as a message with your ranch manager. There have been developments."

"I saw a news alert about the book. I haven't read the story, however."

"Don't."

Finley shut her eyes, her breath leaving her in one long exhale. "That bad, huh?"

"O'Donnell's book is mostly poorly written speculative fiction. Lots of scandalmongering not worth bothering with. No, I'm glad you called because the Justice Department has taken an interest in the insider trading claims. They've opened an investigation." Sadiya paused. "I spoke to my contact. They're being pushed for indictments. Doesn't matter who they find." Her tone carried a warning.

"Okay," Finley said slowly. "But what does that have to do with me?"

"Some of the allegations they're looking at… They involve companies your brother invested in."

"Grayson?" Finley caught her phone from hitting the ground at the last second. She put it back to her ear. "Grayson has nothing to do with this. He never spoke to Barrett about his work for this very reason—"

"I agree there's no fire there. But the O'Donnells

are creating a thick smoke screen. Your brother ran for your father's seat in Congress before abruptly dropping out, despite being far ahead in the polls. He left the country just as Erica was shopping her book. And he's a well-known hedge fund manager with privy access to companies and their senior executives."

"He dropped out of the race for personal reasons! He left the country because he's on his *honeymoon*." Finley hissed the last word. "That is the flimsiest circumstantial evidence ever, and anyone with a brain—"

"I know that. You know that. You also know how the media likes their spin. There is a small but powerful audience out there who support Senator O'Donnell and would like to see him vindicated. The investigators are under pressure to look at all the angles. You're well aware how the game is played."

She was. She was quite good at it, too. But the last five days had cured her of wanting to play games.

She screwed her eyes shut. "So now they're going after Grayson?"

"Don't forget, you're still the ringleader. Grayson merely fed you information, which you then fed to the senator."

Finley scoffed. "Oh yes, however could I forget that. Because I'm the vindictive puppet master who not only led the insider trading ring, but I also set up the ring's members for the fall." She let out a shuddering sigh. "I can't even."

"Erica O'Donnell is skilled at making the media

salivate." Sadiya sounded as disgusted as Finley felt. "I know this isn't the best news, but it's an investigation, not an indictment. They won't find anything."

"An investigation will darken Grayson's reputation. Which is impeccable, by the way, and deservedly so."

"At least the scent appears to be off you."

"Because they're chasing Grayson instead! He doesn't deserve any of this." Her fingernails left deep crescent impressions on her palm.

Sadiya was silent. "We're still trying to shut the whole thing down," she finally said. "There's a possibility it will go away."

"I received a news alert. On my phone screen."

"Right now, the media only possesses innuendo and blind items. O'Donnell's team hasn't named names publicly yet. The best thing to do is sit tight."

"I'm not going anywhere, so that shouldn't be too hard."

Finley finished her conversation with Sadiya and hung up. She flipped her phone over and over in her hands. The prospect of going on the internet had been soured for her. The last thing she wanted to do was to run into gossip sites breathlessly promising the arrival of scurrilous dirt from O'Donnell's memoir.

Staying in the guest suite was also rapidly losing its appeal. She needed to talk to Will—

No. She had not become emotionally dependent on sharing her thoughts with him. She merely wanted to impart a warning he should probably keep quiet about spending five days alone with a member of the notorious Monk family. His investors and shareholders who might not appreciate Will being linked to a DC insider trading scandal.

She'd last seen Will in the kitchen. Halfway there, she could make out his raised voice. She frowned. Will wasn't prone to loud displays of anger. He simmered on slow burn instead. Whatever conversation he was having, it wasn't a happy one.

As she entered the room, his words became clearer. "No! I refuse—" Will had his phone to his ear as he paced, his stiff, angry movements making short work of the vast room. "They can't cancel—"

He turned and saw her. Some of the ferocious energy leaked out of his expression, but he lifted a finger to excuse himself and then left the kitchen. The door to the outside patio slammed shut behind him, ensuring his conversation would remain private.

Great. Looked like their reentry to the real world wasn't going to be a soft landing for either of them.

Will's laptop was precariously perched on the kitchen counter. She walked over, intending to shut the lid and remove the computer to somewhere where it would be less prone to falling. An electronic song trilled from the speakers, announcing an incoming video call from his sister Lauren.

Lauren was one of the owners of Running Coyote and thus her hostess. It would be rude to ignore her, would it not? Plus, Finley had to admit she had some curiosity about Will's sister. He obviously cared deeply about her. And Finley wanted to store up as much data as possible about Will while she could. Her index finger hesitated over the laptop's trackpad, but then she clicked Accept on the call.

The attractive brunette Finley had seen with Will at Grayson's wedding appeared on the screen. She sat in front of a window, the curtains pulled to reveal a dark night sky punctuated with a recognizable city skyline. Lauren was in Tokyo.

"Hi," Finley greeted her. "I'm Finley. Will isn't available but I thought I'd take a message."

"Who did you say you are?" Lauren peered at her screen. "Wait—Grayson's sister, right? Of course. I hope you're enjoying the ranch."

"I am, very much."

"Sorry about Will barging in on your retreat. Nelle and Grayson said you badly needed some me-time. I hope staying with my brother hasn't been too onerous."

Finley kept her expression neutral. "I managed."

Lauren nodded. But there was a gleam in the other woman's gaze that told Finley she might not have been as successful at keeping a straight face as she had hoped. "Good. Listen, Reid has pulled every string he can to get the mudslide cleared as fast as possible. But apparently one of the earthmovers the local crews are using broke down. They're trying to get another one from Los Angeles, but the storm caused a lot of damage up and down the coast."

Finley nodded. "Tim suspected as much. He's done a great job keeping us informed."

"Tim's the best. Are you sure Will isn't available? I really do need to talk to him."

Finley glanced out the kitchen's picture window. Will was pacing, his eyes screwed shut in what looked like frustration. "He's on another call. I could try to interrupt him, but it seems important. I think it's about the EverAftr television series."

"He told you about the series?" Lauren sounded surprised. "Great! So you know."

Finley wasn't sure what Lauren meant, but she wasn't about to tell the other woman that. "I know… It's a tremendous opportunity for him and EverAftr."

"And not just him. Could you take a message for Will after all? It's two in the morning here and I need to get some sleep, or I'd wait until he was free. Tell him Ji-Hoon was admitted to the hospital on Monday and released this morning. He didn't want to alarm Will, but I thought Will should be informed." She rattled off a phone number. "Will has Ji-Hoon's contact info, but just in case, that's the number where Ji-Hoon is staying in Los Angeles."

Finley made a note on her phone. "Got it."

"And tell Will not to worry. Ji-Hoon responded well to treatment. But between us, and the reason I want to talk to Will—I think being part of the series is the only thing keeping Ji-Hoon going. He's so excited to finally have his Hollywood moment." Lauren chuckled. "He said being a producer is better than being an actor. Now he gets to call the shots and crush other people's dreams. He was kidding, of course. But he's like a kid waiting for the candy shop to open."

"I don't blame him. Sounds exciting."

Lauren sobered. "Hopefully production will start soon, for his sake."

Finley nodded. "I'll give Will the message."

"Thanks." Lauren stifled a yawn with her hand. "It was great talking to you. Nelle mentioned you might do a little soul-searching while you were at Running Coyote. I hope the ranch helped you find what you are looking for. It helps me."

Finley's gaze returned to the window, zeroing in on Will as he still paced, his phone pressed against his ear. "Some things became clearer, yes. Thank you, and Reid, for letting me stay here."

Lauren laughed. "I wouldn't thank us, not after all you've been through. You'll have to return when the rains are less torrential."

"It was a freak storm. No worries." She and Lauren said their goodbyes and Finley closed Will's laptop. Her fingertips were still drumming on the computer's lid when Will reentered the kitchen.

Finley drank in his appearance. His navy shirt matched the dark rim outlining his irises. He'd rolled up his sleeves, revealing forearms tanned from helping her muck out the horses' paddocks. He'd exchanged his usual jeans for khakis, to her disappointment. But when he turned his back to her to retrieve a pot from a lower pullout drawer, she decided the khakis provided just as fine a view.

"Oatmeal?" He held up the pot. "I'm craving a hot meal. Anything hot."

"I will never eat a peanut butter sandwich again,"

she agreed. "I hope you don't mind me being nosy, but you seemed rather…perturbed…by your phone call."

"It was nothing." The pot banged on the stove. "Hollywood nonsense."

"It didn't seem like nonsense."

"It will work out. Just takes time, which we have. If I can't leave the ranch, the company can't start production."

"But they can cancel production?" she asked, remembering Will's barked words earlier.

He stirred the oatmeal, clanging the spoon against the sides of the pot. "That's their threat. They're concerned about the marketing if the show isn't built around me. I said they can market the show around real people using a real app to find real love."

"Not a bad description." She was impressed.

"The copywriter whose work you hated wrote that." He threw her an amused look, then began opening and shutting cabinets in a quest for something he couldn't find. "Where's the salt?"

She handed him the shaker, sitting in plain sight on the counter. "What did the production company say to that?"

"That I'm the only real person people will pay a subscription fee to watch using the app. Otherwise, it's not worth their investment." He turned off the heat and ladled the oatmeal into two bowls, handing her one. "Enjoy."

She held the bowl in her both hands, cupping her fingers around its warmth. "In other words, they will cancel the series if you're not in it, because Screenweb thinks the only viable marketing hook is the CEO of EverAftr using his own app to find his match."

He took his bowl into the breakfast room, sitting down at the table with its embroidered tablecloth and collection of cheerful pottery vases serving as a centerpiece. His spoon stabbed into his oatmeal. "We're still talking."

She took the chair opposite him, setting her bowl aside. "Before I forget, your sister called while you were on the phone. A video call, from Tokyo. I answered on your laptop. I hope you don't mind."

"You spoke to Lauren? What did she say?"

"Reid is trying to get the road cleared but there's a lack of equipment, just as Tim said." Finley leaned her elbows on the table, cupping her chin with her hands. She fixed her gaze on Will. "She also wanted to make sure you knew Ji-Hoon was in the hospital. He was released this morning."

Will's spoon stopped halfway to his mouth. He put it down, untouched. "What happened?"

"Lauren didn't say. But…" Finley hesitated. "I got the feeling she didn't think he could wait a long time for production to begin." She reached a hand across the table to Will. "Who is Ji-Hoon?"

"My mentor." Will pushed back his chair. "Would you excuse me? I need to phone Lauren."

"She was going to bed. But I bet she'll take your call if she sees it."

Will walked out of the room, his movements jerky instead of his usual fluid grace. Finley watched him go, then pulled her bowl of oatmeal toward her. The contents were cold. And too salty to eat.

Taking out her phone, she opened the web browser and entered "Will Taylor," "Ji-Hoon" and "EverAftr" into the search bar. Within seconds, she was looking at images of a younger Will—the Will who had occupied her memories for so long. He stood next to an older Asian man in many of the photos, their faces wreathed in smiles.

She clicked on the top link and started to read. It was a profile of Will, written for a business magazine shortly after EverAftr announced the company would be going public. She skimmed, looking for mentions of Ji-Hoon, and quickly found a paragraph quoting Will:

"If Ji-Hoon Park hadn't believed in me when I was struggling after college graduation, EverAftr wouldn't exist. Ji-Hoon was my parents' next-door neighbor. Then his commercial real estate business took off, but our families remained close. While I was growing up, he always showed interest in my school coding projects. He's not a tech guy himself but he knew people in California from having worked in Hollywood as a young man. When he saw I was having a rough time, he made some phone calls. With his contacts, I landed an entry-level position in Santa Monica, a.k.a. Silicon Beach. Things took off from there."

Will had been in California after graduation? She didn't know that. She continued to read.

Things did indeed take off for Taylor. After leav-

ing his job to strike out on his own, he developed a new process for hardware security and sold the patent for a cool million dollars. Other lucrative patent sales followed. But he never forgot his roots in the Chicago area. "I decided to move back to Chicago. I liked SoCal but I missed real pizza, y'know?" he said with a laugh. "And my sisters were complaining they couldn't find the right person using online services. Hookups, sure. But they were tired of constant first dates. They wanted to locate people serious about developing a relationship. Creating a dating app was the last thing on my mind, but Ji-Hoon pointed out it was just a matter of coming up with the right algorithm. He was my first investor. I owe everything to him."

Does Taylor use his own service? The handsome single CEO only laughed when asked—

Finley put down her phone. She'd read enough. Enough to know Will cared deeply about his mentor. And enough to recognize the television series would indeed be a success. The journalist wouldn't have asked if there wasn't public curiosity about the answer.

She drummed her fingers on the tablecloth. No matter how she sliced and diced the variables, only one conclusion could be reached.

Will's mentor eagerly looked forward to being part of the series but his health was precarious. The production company would only move ahead if Will was the main subject of the first season. Therefore, Will needed to be the star.

She must ensure he made it to Los Angeles and in front of the cameras. She had to disabuse him of his silly notions, such as he couldn't pursue his perfect match because he thought he had some sort of obligation to her…or worse, thought he had already found his lifetime partner.

And the clock was ticking on putting Will back on his rightful track, because she'd finally puzzled out what she needed to do once she left the ranch. If the O'Donnell camp was baying for blood to create a diversion from their own transgressions, she'd give it to them. She would dangle herself as bait, to draw any potential attention away from Grayson.

Creating a media frenzy was child's play for her. She'd make Erica O'Donnell look like an amateur by comparison. She knew exactly how to plant a story with enough ambiguous detail to make gossip columnists froth at the mouth. The only difference between this and the work she did as a political campaign manager was that now, she'd be the subject of her own innuendo.

The ranch had been an oasis. She would miss her time here desperately. But as much as she wished she could continue ignoring the outside world, it was time to be proactive. She picked up her phone again and scrolled through her contacts, punching the button to call when she found the right one. "Hey, CC, it's Finley Smythe. Sorry for the last-minute ask, but do you have any availability tomorrow? Can I run an idea past you?"

* * *

Long after sunset, Will walked into the living area to find Finley sitting on the leather sofa closest to the fireplace, the only illumination coming from flames on the hearth. She'd recently showered. Her dark hair was wet and slicked back and she wore a gray hoodie at least three times too big for her. With her legs curled underneath her, she looked like a college student about to burn the midnight oil.

Or a congressional intern, waiting for her date to arrive. His heart turned over in his chest.

"You don't have to sit in the dark now." He turned a nearby lamp on. "Look. Magic."

She smiled, but it didn't reach her eyes. "I've grown accustomed to not having lights. I think I prefer the dark."

He switched the lamp off and sat down beside her. She scooted over to make space, draping herself over the sofa's pillows. A low-energy Finley was unfamiliar to him, and his pulse thumped. "Do you feel okay?" he asked. His hour on the phone with Ji-Hoon learning about his latest medical setback was still very much on his mind. "Not coming down with anything?"

"I'm fine. Just a long day. Lots of excitement." She turned to him. "Finished all your calls? Did they go better than the one this morning?"

Bile rose in the back of his throat at the mention of the phone call. He didn't want the series to be canceled. He knew how much it meant to Ji-Hoon. But it wouldn't be honest to continue with the show's original concept. For one, his answers were all wrong. He thought he wanted a restful life, of low drama and high consistency. A life where he knew what he would be doing a year from now, five years, twenty years. A quiet life, controlled for as few surprises as possible.

Life with Finley would never be quiet. Predictability would be thrown out the window.

He couldn't think of anything better.

But first, he needed to get past her determination to keep their current situation entanglement-free. "The last call was with the exec team at EverAftr. Different type of stress. More enjoyable. Were you able to reach everyone you wanted to talk to?"

"Yes." She kept her gaze focused on the drawstrings of her hoodie as she tied and untied them. "Why didn't you study law as you planned?"

Where did that question come from? He shrugged. "Three years of graduate school is expensive. I took a job instead."

"That's the only reason?" Her gaze searched his.

He rubbed his temple. "The idea lost its appeal. Decided to do something else."

"Did our summer have something to do with why it lost its appeal? Did I?"

"Why are you asking?" He shifted on the sofa so he could catch her gaze, but her eyes were unreadable. "As I've said previously, things turned out okay."

She leaned her head against the cushions. "I think you gave up your dream because someone or something made you feel small. So, you left Washington and politics, never to return. And I believe that some-one was me."

"Lee." His beautiful, capricious and far-too-perceptive-for-her-own-good Lee. "If anyone made me feel bad about myself, that was my fault. I let them get to me."

"But it doesn't work that way, does it? We can't help but be affected by other people. We're human. We're social animals. We crave contact with others."

His eyebrows flew up to nearly hit his hairline. "I agree. But I'm surprised to hear you say it."

"Why?"

"You don't do relationships. No attachments." He stretched his legs along the sofa's length, and then tugged Finley to lie down next to him. After a mo-ment of resistance, she joined him. The sofa was just wide enough for them both, Finley reclining half on, half off him. "I thought I'd never get you to acknowl-edge people need each other. Glad to hear you've fi-nally come around."

He felt more than heard her chuckle. "I didn't say that. I said people can't help but affect one another."

He was certainly affected by her. But although his blood kindled as always at her nearness, he was con-tent to hold her and listen to her words in the dark. "It's not the same thing?"

"No." She lifted her head. "Did I affect you so badly you gave up your dream?"

He tightened his arms around her. "It was my choice to give up on law school. Not your choice, not anyone else's. Mine. But if you're asking if you hurt me? Yes. The breakup hurt."

"I know." She kissed his cheek, then laid her head back on his chest. "If you hadn't been caught in the rainstorm and stranded on the ranch, you'd be working on the first episode of the series now, correct?"

He frowned. "Probably. Or getting close to it. But that ship has sailed. Why do you ask?"

"Just trying to figure something out."

"Like what?"

She shook her head. "Nothing important. Just idle curiosity." Her fingers began to trace a pattern over his shoulders, across his collarbone and back again. Feather-light, her touch trailed sparks in its wake. "This is nice, isn't it?"

"Very." The comfy sofa, the crackle and hiss of the fire and Finley curled up tight against him—he couldn't think of anywhere else he wanted to be. "But I'm still wondering what prompted this conversation."

She didn't respond with words. Instead, she kissed the side of his neck, her mouth hot and wet against his skin. Her hands began to travel lower, finding the button of his waistband, the zipper of his fly. With a supreme effort, he sat up, gathering her to him so he could deposit her to sit next to him. She stared at him, her gaze wide with surprise. "What? Did I miss something? Was this a date, so there's an obligation to talk first?"

"You use sex when you don't want to have a conversation."

She folded her arms across her chest. "Really."

"In my observation."

She huffed. "Let's say you're right, which you're not. Most men would view that as a positive."

"I'm not saying it isn't. But not when you're obviously holding something back that is bothering you."

She rolled her eyes. "I can't believe you'd rather talk than have sex, but okay. Here's what I've been mulling all day. What's going to happen after you leave Running Coyote?"

"You mean when *we* leave."

"Fine. When we leave."

"We—" he stressed the word again "—will figure it out."

She shook her head. "Not good enough. You have a company to run. A TV series. You must have a plan in mind."

This was his fault for not letting her have her way with him as she intended. Served him right. But they needed to have this discussion, and the sooner, the better. The road wouldn't stay closed for long. "I do."

"Good." She nodded.

"Involving you."

Her nod came slower. "Okay."

"And me."

"Since it's your plan, I would hope so."

"Together. As we should have been all along."

She inhaled, but her arms remained loose by her sides. She didn't jump up and run. He considered that a win. "And the series?" she asked.

"Using the app on camera to find a romantic partner would be a lie. I have no desire to date anyone else." He leaned over and kissed her. She didn't respond at first. Then she sighed and kissed him back. He broke contact and held her gaze with his. "So. I won't do it."

She blinked, but not before he saw the shimmer of moisture at the corner of her eyes. "But what about your mentor? Ji-Hoon? Isn't he involved with the series? What if they decide the cost of production won't be worth their investment unless you're the star, and they pull the plug?"

He swallowed. Damned Screenweb executives, refusing to compromise. If they would only see reason. But the show wasn't canceled yet. Ji-Hoon could still have his Hollywood dream. "Yes, he has a producer credit. But I'm confident we can find a way forward."

"You're so optimistic. Which is not the same as realistic." She bit her lower lip.

He took her chin in his left hand, keeping their gazes locked. "There's only one nonnegotiable item. I want to be with you. I know we've been together only five days. But in some ways, it's been fifteen years."

He knew better than to mention love. Finley had made her opinion on the subject very clear.

But as she'd alluded to earlier, they affected one another. She'd focused on the pain of their past, but he chose to look ahead. *Affect*, after all, was the root of the word *affection*. And affection was just the start of what he felt for her. How he'd always felt.

Her dark eyes were wide, filled with an emotion he couldn't quite name. She pulled back from his touch, escaping into the shadows. "What if I told you I don't want the same thing?" Her voice was a thin whisper in the darkness. "Would you do the show then?"

"Then tell me." He threw his arms open. "Tell me you don't want me. Although your actions a few minutes ago said otherwise."

"Of course I want you. But what if it's only for a night? And we part forever the next day." Her voice grew stronger. "Would you star in the series then?"

"No. Because I'd find you the next night. And ask you to tell me again you don't want me." He grinned at her. "I'll take my chances on getting the same answer." He pushed up her sleeve to reveal her sensitive inner elbow, caressing the spot that always made her shudder. "I like my odds."

Her laugh became a voluptuous sigh. "Damn it, Will. I have zero self-control where you are concerned. Remember later, I tried to give you an easy out."

Before he could puzzle out what she meant, Finley had slipped off the sofa to kneel between his legs. She pulled his head down to meet hers and her tongue swept into his mouth as she tugged on his shirt, sending at least one button flying. But even as the heat and the pressure began to build, Will discerned a difference in their lovemaking. Her eyes remained open. Her movements were slower, more deliberate.

It was if she were memorizing every detail. As if this were truly their last night together.

Then her lips lowered onto their target, and he stopped thinking.

Thirteen

Finley was in Trudy's paddock when she heard the helicopter. She gave Trudy an apple, then buried her face in the mare's neck, inhaling the scent of dusty hay and warm horse. "This is it, girl," she whispered to the mare. "Wish me luck. Don't worry, I'll be back later for your supper."

She petted Trudy's nose, then walked over to the fence that separated the mare's paddock from Ranger's. The gelding's dark eyes watched her as she approached. "Don't give me that stare," she said, shining another apple on her jeans leg before holding it out for Ranger to munch. "This is the right thing to do. He's going to thank me for this, one day. He's going to look at his beautiful wife and amazing children and be oh so glad he didn't let a mudslide ruin his future."

Ranger tossed his head and snorted. "Yeah, I knew you'd take his side. You men stick together. But honestly, this is for the best."

The sound of rotor blades grew louder. She turned and watched as the MD500 copter came into view, descending until it hovered, looking for a good spot to land. Running Coyote had a helipad near the base camp, but it was on the other side of the mudslide. The helicopter's pilot finally settled on a flat stretch of the lawn below the pool.

She walked toward the house, steeling herself for what was to come. But before she could reach the door, Will came racing out. He grabbed her and placed her behind him, as if to shield her from whatever was in the copter.

"What the—where did that come from?" he shouted. "I'm going to go call Tim."

She stopped him from reentering the house. The rotors slowed, the wind died down and the noise subsided, allowing her to speak at a normal volume. "There's no need to call Tim. I hired the helicopter."

Shock froze Will's features. "You did what?"

"I hired it. A friend owns a helicopter sightseeing operation. I pulled in a big favor."

"But why?" Confusion filled his gaze, followed rapidly by hurt. "You're leaving?"

She hardened her heart against the pain in his eyes and shook her head. "No. I'm not leaving. You are."

He stared at her. "I don't understand."

"See the pilot exiting the cockpit? The tall Black

woman? That's my friend CC." CC turned and helped a passenger out the door. "And the man—"

"Ji-Hoon," Will breathed. He turned to her. "You brought Ji-Hoon here? Why?"

She kissed him on his cheek, storing up the sensation of his unshaven stubble against her lips, pulling away before she was tempted to linger forever. "You're going to Los Angeles. This is goodbye."

"What? Lee, what are you doing?"

She swallowed. She had to get her words out fast. "Ji-Hoon and CC will reach us soon, so I'm only going to say this once. You must do the series. That was what you wanted. Your big goal. And then the mudslide interfered and caused a bump in your journey. But that's all our time here on the ranch was. An aberration. A detour. So—"

"Stop. Before you say something we'll both regret for another fifteen years."

She shook her head. She never cried. But for the first time in a very long while, she wanted to. "That summer, I listened to Barrett. I made you feel less than, because I thought our relationship was conditional, that you were attracted more to my family's status than to me. That calling us 'soul mates' was just a verbal trick, so you could get what you wanted." She sniffed. No, she wouldn't cry. "And because of that, you gave up on your dream career. I won't let you derail your life now."

She threw out her arms. "You want to settle down with a partner and start a family, or you would've never agreed to the series. So go find her, Will. Go find the woman you're meant to be with."

"No." His head shook, a blur too rapid to follow. "No. Because she's right here. And you know that. You might not like the word *love*, but that's what this is. That's what we have. That's what we always had."

She laughed. It was only a trick of her ear that made it sound like a sob. "We have good sex. We're compatible in bed. The last week was nothing more than two consenting adults, trapped without television or internet, who made the most of a bad situation."

"You don't believe that."

No. She didn't. But she needed him to believe she did. "Being with you was great. Really great. Best sex I've had in years, and I thank you for that. But you have a life and I have a life and it's time to stop pretending the real world doesn't exist. You have an obligation to the production company—"

His hands clenched. "You can't want me to be in the series. We spoke about this, last night."

Want was a strong word. It implied so many things. But ultimately, her wants were selfish. They didn't matter. Not when it came to his future.

She raised her chin. "If you ask me if I want you, I'll always say yes. But that's sex."

"It's more. I love you, Lee. And you love me. You're too stubborn to admit it."

He said he loved her. Her lungs couldn't get enough air. Funny, the one time she wanted strings wrapped tightly around a relationship was the one time that just wasn't possible. She couldn't hold his gaze any longer, or he might see how much she longed to say the words back.

So instead, she scoffed. "Hey, I'm flattered you think a week of great sex is worth throwing away millions of dollars and your potential future happiness, but one of us needs to be logical. You have a company. You have shareholders. The series is going to make them lots of money. People depend on you." She indicated Ji-Hoon, who was slowly making his way across the lawn toward them with CC's assistance. "And I have my own commitments."

His gaze narrowed dangerously. "Such as?"

She took a much-needed deep breath. "Preparing for an insider trading investigation, for one. Senator O'Donnell's wife has accused me of being the ringleader of the current Washington scandal du jour. The press will have the story soon."

Surprise mixed into the emotions rapidly cycling in his expression. "Insider trading allegations? You never said anything—"

"Why would I ruin the fantasy of the last few days with sordid details? But it's another reason why we must go our separate ways. Now, before the media catches on we spent the week trapped together at Running Coyote." She cut him off with a shake of her head. "I know how gossip works. You want attention for EverAftr and your series, but not that type of attention. The sleazy type does no one any good."

Through her peripheral vision she could see Ji-Hoon and CC coming closer. They would be in range to overhear her discussion with Will at any minute.

She pulled out her last weapon, plastering a wide smile on her face and giving him an airy shrug. "We had a good run these last few days. But relationships based on intense experiences—like being stranded on a ranch thanks to a mudslide—never work." His gaze remained darkly incandescent without a glimmer of recognition. She knew he wouldn't get the film reference. Instead of annoying her, his refusal to learn pop culture history only reminded her much she lov—no. How much she enjoyed being with him. Which made her next statement even harder to say. "And so we move on to bigger and better things. I'll always remember our time here on the ranch fondly, but we're done."

He staggered, just a step, as the echo of the words she used to break up with him the first time resonated. She planted her feet, preparing to hold her ground. He would briefly argue with her, like he did fifteen years ago. But then he would turn angry, say things that would forever be painfully carved on her soul and walk away.

But to her shock, the fury drained out of his gaze, replaced by something like…pity. And deep, deep affection. He cupped her cheek with his hand and her pulse stuttered.

"You're scared," he said. "You're afraid someone will find you lovable, so you strike first and drive them away. And I get why, now. Your father left. Barrett was an ass who taught you relationships were transactional. No one protected you so you protect yourself. And you protect others. Like me. You're doing this to protect me. Because you love me."

His words hit her heart like so many needle-nosed darts. Every cell she possessed wanted to run away from the truth, hanging in the air between them. His gaze kept her pinned in place, demanding she admit he was right.

He stepped closer, the wind carrying his scent to her, his hand on her cheek bringing warmth. "I can take care of myself. And if you allow me, I can help with the insider trading allegations. Give us time so we can find a way forward. For both of us."

For an eye blink, she allowed herself to relax into his touch. But while the picture he painted was very tempting, she knew what he proposed just wasn't possible. His optimism was no match for reality.

She pulled away, folding her arms as she called up her smirk. "A guy runs a dating app and suddenly he's an expert in human psychology."

He shook his head. "No. But I know you—"

"Oh, you know me. You know me better than I know myself, right?" Anger kindled in her belly, and she welcomed its glow. Anything to drive away the cold emptiness that threatened to consume her. "Sorry, unlike you I don't confuse orgasms with love. Now, CC will fly you and Ji-Hoon to Los Angeles—"

Sparks of answering anger lit his gray-blue gaze. "Ji-Hoon is ill. You shouldn't have pulled him into your scheme—"

"He was excited when I asked him, and his doctors gave permission. Someone must remind you what you have at stake here, and he's your mentor. I knew after our conversation last night you'd never listen to me."

"You're so afraid of future happiness you can't see—"

She waved him off, her hand oscillating rapidly. "What future happiness? Investigations and scandals? That's what I have in store. But you don't. I'm offering you an express pass to get back to the life you had planned before a freak storm stranded you here. Take it, damn it." She pushed past him.

He reached for her arm, his hand gently holding her bicep. "Unlike last time, I know what you're doing. You're trying to arrange all the pieces on your own. Don't walk away. Talk to me. Let me help."

She turned around. With supreme effort, she made herself look him in the eye. "Unlike last time, no one is manipulating me. I'm saying goodbye out of my own volition. Please respect that."

He dropped her arm, allowing her to pass. His gaze burned a hole through the back of her jacket.

She continued down the stairs of the terrace, her left hand outstretched in greeting as the newcomers reached her. She relaxed her expression into a grin, hoping her flushed cheeks would be attributed to the brisk February air. "Hi, I'm Finley. You must be Ji-Hoon. I hope you had a good flight. But of course you did. CC is a great pilot."

Ji-Hoon's handshake was firm, his smile warm and genuine. Finley liked him immediately. But his gaze was shrewd as he glanced between her and Will, still standing motionless on the terrace. Intuition told her the sooner she made herself scarce, the fewer pointed questions she might have to answer. "So!" She clapped her hands together. "I'll let you catch up with Will as he packs. CC, when do you need to take off for Los Angeles?"

"I'm leaving to refuel the chopper. I'll be back to pick up everyone in, say, an hour?" She addressed Ji-Hoon. "You'll be good to go by then?"

"I'll be good, but it's not up to me." He turned to Finley. "What about you?"

"Oh, I'm not leaving. Not with you and Will." She laughed, a high tinkle that made her cringe inside as soon as it came out of her mouth. "I have to care for the horses until the ranch manager is able to take over. And speaking of the horses, I hope you'll excuse me. I need to give them their exercise. If I'm not back before you leave, it was lovely to meet you."

"The pleasure is all mine." The twinkle in his eyes diminished, but the warmth in his smile remained. "Thank you for the opportunity to spend quality time with Will before the chaos breaks loose."

"My pleasure. I know you have a lot of catching up to do." She threw a glance at Will, who stayed statue-still where she left him through the flurry of the arrivals. Finally, he came forward to thump Ji-Hoon on the back, shaking CC's hand.

His gaze continued to singe whenever he glanced at her, leaving smoking holes behind.

As Will escorted Ji-Hoon into the house, she escaped to the stable. She saddled up Ranger and then gave him his head, letting him take her wherever he wanted to go. She refused to look back at the house.

She wouldn't have seen anything, anyway. Her vision was too clouded by tears.

Will stopped packing, his attention caught by movement outside the window of his room. Finley was galloping away on Ranger without a backward glance. One thing was for sure: he was never coming back to the ranch, no matter how many times Lauren and Reid invited him. How could he when every square inch would remind him of her?

He turned back to his open suitcase on top of the bed and threw more clothes in it, not caring where they landed.

"That bad, huh?" Ji-Hoon asked from his chair in the corner.

"Afraid so." Will slammed the top of the suitcase closed and zipped it up. "What did Finley say when she called you?"

"She said the two of you had been trapped for almost a week and you would appreciate new company from an old friend."

Will scoffed and shook his head. "Nothing about the TV series?"

"Just that you were working on ideas. She made it sound like you were eager to catch up on lost time, which is why she suggested I fly up here." Ji-Hoon shrugged. "I would never say no to a helicopter ride from Los Angeles to Santa Barbara. The scenery is breathtaking."

Will pushed the suitcase to the side and sat down on the bed, catching Ji-Hoon's gaze. "I can't be the subject of the series. But if they can't build the marketing around the CEO of EverAftr using his own app to look his partner, Screenweb will probably cancel production. I don't want to disappoint you."

Ji-Hoon nodded. "Well, being a TV producer would have been fun. I was looking forward to having dinner at Spago—is Spago around? It was all the rage in the eighties. Everyone in the industry went there."

"Still popular, I hear."

"There you go. But I don't have be a TV producer to have a meal, do I?"

"Pretty sure anyone with a reservation can eat there."

"Good. Then that's the plan. We'll go to Spago. The rest is gravy."

Will's gaze was caught by a sparkle of gold from under the bed. He bent down to retrieve the object. It was Finley's shoe from the night they had their date in the library.

Man, his chest hurt. His ribs were simultaneously too tight for his lungs but too big for his heart, bouncing painfully around the cavernous space. He looked up at Ji-Hoon. "Should I stay, try to talk more sense into her? Or should I go?"

Ji-Hoon raised his eyebrows. "I don't know. I just met her. Her friend CC is very nice, however."

Will carefully put the shoe on top of the chest of drawers. "I know why she's running away. I don't know how to make her stop."

"Probably shouldn't make her do anything."

"Bad choice of words." There was a sharp pain below his sternum. No matter how he shifted, it would not go away. "I love her. I've loved her since I was twenty-one."

"Twenty-one...hmm. So, she's the woman you met during your internship in DC." Ji-Hoon regarded him. "You were very hurt."

Somehow, today both did and didn't hurt as bad as the first breakup. "I was much younger. I had less perspective then." *Damn it, Lee.* He wished they'd had more time. More time to show her how much he cared. More time to prove to her that what they had was the stuff poets declaimed and songwriters sung about. But even if they'd been trapped on the ranch for a century, it might not have been enough. Finley's defenses were high and deep. "But I don't feel awesome now, either."

"Unrequited love is painful."

Will shook his head. "It's not unrequited. I'm positive of that. But things are...complicated." The allegations she alluded to still stunned him. "You lectured on real estate at the University of Chicago's business school. I don't suppose you know anyone there who's an expert on insider trading?"

"Insider trading? That is a complication."

"Finley isn't a rule follower." The memory of climbing over a fence to enjoy a midnight assignation in a private Washington garden flashed through his head, and he smiled. "But a crook? No."

"Then I suppose the question is, how do you un-complicate things?"

Will stared out the window again. Finley was long gone, disappeared into the brush-filled hills. "She asked me to respect her decision."

And he received the impression that if he stayed and tried to talk more sense into her she would only stonewall him further—using heavy stones with very sharp edges. He turned to Ji-Hoon. "I'll return to Los Angeles with you. Give her one less complication to worry about."

The last week had been an intense maelstrom of emotion. He understood why she was determined to put space between them.

Plus, she wasn't wrong. He did have responsibilities and commitments. Big ones, with people's livelihoods riding on them. They required his attention.

But he wasn't walking away for good. Not this time. The mistake he'd made fifteen years ago was to not demonstrate to Finley that his love for her was deeper and stronger than her doubts about herself.

He'd give her the room for which she asked. But not enough that she would be lost to him for good. He hoped.

Fourteen

Finley pulled back the curtains, just the tiniest fraction, to check on the setup for the press conference. The stage of the auditorium at Sadiya's law firm held a long table with two chairs behind it: one for her, centered in the middle, and one next to her for Sadiya. Microphones and recorders were already arranged at the front of the table, while cameras on tripods lined the back wall. Some people were milling about, conversing in groups of two or three, but most of the seats facing the stage were empty. Which was as expected since she wasn't scheduled to face the media for another thirty minutes.

She let the curtain fall back into place and faced her sister-in-law, who was shaking her head. "I can't believe you played the 'I'm breaking up with you for your own good' card," Nelle said. "You and Grayson—what is with you two? He did the same thing to me." She pointed to the wedding band on the fourth finger of her left hand. "Here's a hint. That excuse doesn't stick."

Finley resumed perusing photos on Nelle's cell phone. Nelle and Grayson had returned from their two-month extended honeymoon several weeks ago, having had such a good time in Kenya that they added other African countries as well as a good swath of Europe to their itinerary. But when they touched down in San Francisco, Finley had been busy closing her DC apartment. She'd sublet it after Barrett was indicted, believing she would eventually return to the Hill in some capacity or another. Finally, she'd decided to permanently relocate back to California. Easier to wait for the other shoe to drop with family nearby.

But harder to erase her memories of Will. Every time someone mentioned Santa Barbara, or Napa, or driving down the coast, thoughts of him flooded her being. She missed him even more than the first time they parted. Regret was a painful companion.

Her only consolation was knowing she'd made the right call and Will was back on his intended path. She'd found Screenweb's press release announcing the start of production while scrolling through the internet shortly after she left the ranch, late at night when she couldn't sleep.

At least the sticky morass of Erica O'Donnell's accusations kept her mind somewhat occupied and not constantly dwelling on Will. O'Donnell's memoir had sold at auction for a sizable sum and had been rushed to the printer. While the book had yet to hit the stores, juicy excerpts had been leaked all over the mediasphere.

Today's press conference was part of Finley's plan to keep the media's attention focused on her and off any allegations that might come Grayson's way. When Nelle heard about the event, she volunteered to keep Finley company backstage until Finley and Sadiya went in front of the cameras. Finley accepted, both to keep her nerves at bay and to assuage Nelle's persistent curiosity about Finley's stay at Running Coyote in person, a conversation she had avoided until now.

She held up Nelle's phone so Nelle could see what she was looking at. "Why didn't you update your social media more often while you were in Kenya? Some of these shots are amazing."

"You should see the pictures Grayson took with his SLR camera… But you're trying to change the subject. Why on earth did you break up with Will like that?"

"My situation is not comparable to what happened between you and Grayson." Finley started counting on her fingers. "One, Grayson has always been a hopeless romantic, although I have no idea where he got it from. Certainly not from hanging out with me. Two, you had a fairy godmother, if I do say so myself. Not to take full credit, but I had something to do with your reunion. Three, it's a stretch to call this a breakup when we spent less than a week together— can you really break up after a handful of days? Four,

I didn't do it for his own good. I did it because it was the right thing to do."

Nelle regarded her. "Uh-huh," she deadpanned.

Finley mock-rolled her eyes at Nelle and gave the phone back to her. "Thanks for coming. I appreciate it."

"Grayson is on his way."

"I'm concerned about Sadiya. She should be here by now." She checked her own phone. No missed calls, texts or voice mails.

Nelle placed a gentle hand on Finley's arm. "You've got this. The press conference is a walk in the park for you."

Finley examined her fingers, looking for flaws in her new manicure. Always important to look one's best when facing a firing squad of journalists. "Sadiya and I have a pretty good strategy. I hope she gets here soon."

She started to pace. They were expecting a full house, thanks to Erica O'Donnell's recent appearances on TV talk shows to promote her book. The noise grew louder from the other side of the curtain as time ticked down.

She and Sadiya planned to issue vague statements, backed with innuendo, to make it appear as if Finley did indeed have knowledge of the insider trading scheme. By indicating there might be blood in the water, the media sharks would be drawn to circling her while the investigation was ongoing. Finley wasn't concerned the investigators would uncover anything; there was nothing to find. But enough tantalizing inconclusive statements would be dripped to keep all eyes tightly on her. And off anyone else.

No matter the outcome of the investigation, after today her professional reputation would be ruined even more than it already was. It was a consequence she was prepared to face. And it was yet more proof that she'd made the right decision at Running Coyote. If she and Will had continued their relationship, the stench would be on him, too. It always carried over. She was in this predicament in the first place because the stink of Barrett's scandal made her an easy target for Erica O'Donnell's accusations.

Loud, excited conversation began to buzz from the other side of the curtain. The scrape of chairs and the sounds of people scrambling to leave the auditorium were easy to identify. Finley and Nelle exchanged confused looks. "What's going on out there?" Nelle asked.

The two women were about to pull back the curtain to see for themselves when Sadiya swept into the backstage space. Her dark brown eyes sparkled. "Change of plans, everyone!"

Finley whirled about. "You're here! What change? Why are people leaving?"

"Oh, a few will stay behind to get your reaction." Sadiya handed Finley an electronic tablet. On the screen was a headline in big, bold capital letters: "GAME OVER FOR SEN. O'DONNELL, WIFE." Underneath, the subheadline read, "Feds indict former Washington power couple for selling government secrets, insider trading."

Finley looked up. "When did this happen?"

Sadiya gave her a smug grin. "Just now. Literally hot off the presses."

"Does this mean what I think it means?" Finley didn't dare allow herself to hope. Hope was flimsy and led to crushed expectations.

"It means the O'Donnells were hoisted on their own petard. They went to their dark web friends to falsify transactions so Erica's accusations would stick more firmly. But what they didn't know? The friend they approached to hack into various accounts to cover their tracks was working undercover for the FBI."

"Wow."

"It gets better. The Securities and Exchange Commission can take months, even years to investigate allegations. But your case received priority. That's the reason why I was late. I was pushing to get an answer as to what we could reveal at the press conference. My contact said they knew you and your brother were in the clear weeks ago, but they wanted to give the feds time to finish their dark web investigation and not tip off the O'Donnells. Timing worked out perfectly, I must say."

"We were cleared weeks ago?" Finley tried closing her mouth. It only fell open again.

"Unofficially, yes, but it wasn't confirmed. Officially, no, not until the indictments could be announced. I didn't know, either, until today."

"I can't believe the investigation was over so fast."

Sadiya shrugged. "It seems someone likes you.

My contact said you should thank someone named Ji-Hoon Park for the expedited investigation. Apparently, he knows one of the SEC unit chiefs from their days lecturing together at the University of Chicago."

"Wait. Grayson was under suspicion?" Nelle broke into the conversation. "And you knew?" She turned to Finley, balling her fists on her hips.

"I…" Finley blindly reached out her hand, seeking a chair, a wall, anything to keep her propped upright. Ji-Hoon interceded on her behalf? How did he… Will must have said something. But…why would he…

"You knew?" Nelle repeated, dark clouds brewing in her gaze. "Fin, you should have told us. I couldn't figure out why you insisted on putting this display on for the media, but now I get it. You're doing that thing again, where you try to manufacture outcomes without letting the people affected know."

"Hey, everything turned out okay," Finley said.

"That's not an excuse! You may have all the good intentions in the world, but you can't continue thinking you can manipulate your way out of every situation on your own. Stop treating the word 'help' like it's one of the bad four-letter words."

Finley shivered at the echoes of Will's last words to her in Nelle's accusations. Was that what was she doing? Manipulating others?

Like how Barrett manipulated her?

Affecting the people she loved, but to their detriment?

She had always suspected she and Barrett were alike. But she didn't have to be like him. Perhaps if

Barrett had asked for help, confided in the people who loved him, he wouldn't have turned to fraud to maintain appearances.

There was a lesson in there, somewhere, for her.

She turned to Sadiya. "What do I do next? I was preparing myself to be a punch line on late night talk shows for months to come. You ruined my plans."

"Make new ones." Sadiya shrugged and looked at her watch. "Ready to go face the media? Or whoever is left?"

"Can I have a minute?" Finley tried to collect her thoughts. But they had scattered far beyond her reach. As soon as she pinned one down, another struggled loose and flitted away.

Ji-Hoon had called in a favor for a woman he barely met. He must have done it because Will asked him to. But why? She'd all but told him to stay out of her life. Sure, she said what she did to give him his future back, but still. As Nelle just said, intentions were not excuses. And when she'd returned to the ranch after her long ride on Ranger to find every trace of his presence gone, she thought he'd taken her words at face value.

She'd expected her relationship with Will to return to the status quo of the past fifteen years: radio silence with zero contact. That's what she'd geared her heart up to anticipate. Those were the walls she'd built around her expectations. And yet...

She took out her phone, clicked on her email app and scrolled down.

An invite sat in her inbox, from an email account with a Screenweb address. She opened it for the first time since it arrived ten days ago. It contained an offer for a VIP all-access pass to the launch party for Screenweb's summer series, to be held in LA in one week's time. *Finding EverAftr* was listed among their new debuts.

The attached note read simply, "Since you were so insistent that the series go forward, I thought you might like an advanced look at the first episodes. Please arrive by 7:30 p.m. Will."

Before she could do the cowardly thing and delete the entire email, she clicked Accept on the invite. She owed Will and Ji-Hoon her thanks for the expeditated investigation in person. Besides, she'd told Will to go out and find his perfect match. She was glad he'd listened. She only prayed it wouldn't be too painful to witness how happy he was without her.

But a slender candle of optimism remained lit, despite all her efforts to snuff it out. Perhaps hope wasn't as fragile as she thought. Will wasn't cruel. He didn't send her the invite just to rub a new relationship in her face. He must have another reason for wanting her there. Whatever his motivation may be.

She grabbed Nelle's hand. "I'm sorry. You were right. Someone once told me I protect others because I didn't have much protection growing up. And as a result, I also do all I can to push people away, to not let them in. I should have told you and Grayson. We're lucky my scheme to draw all the attention didn't blow up in our faces. I promise, next time I'm accused of nefarious dealings, you two will be my first call."

She turned to Sadiya. "I'm ready. Let's go kick some media butt."

* * *

Palm trees swung high overhead but didn't block the bright Los Angeles sun. The rays beat down on the red carpet, which rolled from the street to the entrance of a hip, trendsetting downtown hotel. Will sucked in a breath as the door of his limousine was opened. Ji-Hoon exited from the car pulling up behind him. They met where the carpet began. "Do you think she'll show up?" Will asked his mentor.

"The Screenweb publicist said she RSVP'd," Ji-Hoon reminded him. "I did just receive a beautiful thank you basket for allegedly helping to nudge along the SEC investigation. But my phone call wouldn't have moved the needle."

"Speaking of the publicist, here she is." Will smiled as a young woman approached, dressed in the obligatory black suit worn by young Hollywood execs despite the unseasonably warm late May afternoon.

The publicist greeted him and Ji-Hoon, and then spoke into her headset. "Secured the talent. Walking now."

"Talent," Ji-Hoon whispered to Will. "Finally. I'm talent."

The publicist turned to Will and indicated a small stage halfway down the red carpet, surrounded by a banner of repeated Screenweb logos printed on a white background. "The step and repeat is just ahead. You'll take some photos, but most of the press is gathered upstairs on the pool deck for the party. At six o'clock, the president of Screenweb will make a few announcements, and we'll roll the teaser footage from the new series. *Finding EverAftr* is scheduled to be last. After that, you'll take some questions from journalists, and then you're free to mingle with the guests. There's a VIP area for when you need an escape. Are you ready?"

Will's gaze searched the crowd gathered to watch the celebrity arrivals. He was far from the biggest name at the presentation and most of the people ignored him in favor of another new arrival, an aging screen legend making a comeback in a historical drama series.

Finley was nowhere to be seen.

"Lead on," he said to the publicist, affecting a smile he didn't feel.

Will posed in front of the banner, feeling somewhat foolish, but didn't trip over his own feet while walking on the rather lumpy red carpet, which he considered a success. Ji-Hoon thoroughly enjoyed his time bantering with the photographers, and even stole attention away from the movie star.

They were whisked up in a hotel elevator that opened directly onto a rooftop pool deck, which had been reserved exclusively for the event. A well-stocked bar occupied one side of the wall next to the elevator, while clear glass railings outlined the rest of the desk. Wide-screen high-definition monitors were attached to poles dotted around the venue, ensuring the cocktail-attired guests had an unobstructed view of the Screenweb promos running on a constant loop. The skyscrapers of Los Angeles provided a spectacular backdrop.

Ji-Hoon rubbed his hands together as they stepped on the deck. "I'm going to find a nonalcoholic cocktail and schmooze. Want to take bets on when the first guest goes into the pool?"

"With luck, after I'm back at the corporate apartment." Will grinned. No matter what happened, he would always be glad Ji-Hoon had enjoyed his time working with Will on the series.

"So, nine thirty." Ji-Hoon made a note on his phone, then tossed Will a wave. "Ciao, as they say in the industry."

"You mean Italy."

"You have much to learn about this town, my friend." Ji-Hoon plunged into the crowd.

Once Will was alone, he turned his back on the view to take in the guests. The deck was filling rapidly, the guests dressed in anything from sharp, European-tailored suits to khaki shorts topped with Hawaiian-print shirts, while others wore sequined dresses verging on ball gowns or even ripped jeans and tank tops. He recognized some people. Eduardo Cabrillo, the star of ScreenWeb's breakout sword-and-sorcery fantasy series, was unmistakable with his waist-length hair. And the beautiful woman with the glowing ebony skin could only be Amanda Gbeho, currently appearing in a perfume ad on billboards all over LA. More than once, Will squinted at someone and almost approached them to ask if they had gone to high school together, only to realize the person he was staring at had played the next-door neighbor on

Lauren's favorite sitcom or had been a featured player in a film an old girlfriend had dragged him to.

Thinking about films made him recall Finley's teasing admonishments regarding his lack of movie knowledge. He tensed, his stomach rebelling against the champagne he'd tasted in the limo only to leave the glass mostly untouched. All these famous faces packing the party, but the one face he wanted to see was nowhere to be found.

The music wafting through the speakers stopped, and the president of Screenweb stepped onto the low dais at the far end of the pool deck, the setting sun casting a golden glow over the scene. Will continued to watch the crowd, his gaze zeroing in on the elevator whenever it opened to spill out more guests, as the president introduced one new summer series after another.

Then the theme song they'd chosen for *Finding EverAftr* began to play. Will dragged his attention back to the stage. His heartbeat thudded in his ears, a dull ache.

She hadn't come to the party.

The president caught Will's eye and motioned him forward, taking the microphone off its stand as Will approached. "Folks, I'm going to mix things up for our last great series. Instead of listening to me describe it, we're going to let you hear directly from someone intimately involved in the show. And when I say intimate, I mean it." He chuckled along with the audience's knowing laughter. "Without further ado, here's the CEO of EverAftr and the executive producer of our new series based on the globally popular app, Will Taylor!"

Will's feet carried him toward the dais, moving on autopilot. He thought he'd braced himself for the disappointment he'd experience should she not show up, but the crushing agony as his optimism died an excruciating death was beyond his limited imagination. Still, he shook the president's hand and took the microphone from him, pausing for one moment to deeply inhale and push down his heartache.

Then, from out the corner of his eye, he saw someone pushing through the crowd. The person beelined toward the stage, bursting through the first row to stand directly in front of him.

Finley.

Her dark hair was longer, the ends softly curling around her shoulders. She wore a plain blue dress but what the silky fabric did to her curves was anything but simple. Sophisticated but hinting at immeasurable pleasures in the dark; her outfit suited her to a T. Her golden brown eyes were wide with apology, her cheeks flushed pink.

He'd never seen anyone more beautiful, including at tonight's party filled wall to wall with photogenic celebrities.

She mouthed, "Sorry I'm late," followed by a roll of her eyes and the word, "traffic."

He wanted to laugh. No, actually, he wanted to sing. Or perhaps dance. And those two activities had never crossed his mind as things he should do before. Now he understood why people liked musicals. If he could belt out a song about how seeing Finley made him feel, he would.

The Screenweb president raised his eyebrows in Will's direction, and the publicist threw him a confused look. Right, he was supposed to be talking, not staring at the vision that was Finley, here, almost within arm's reach. He brought the microphone to his mouth. He wouldn't deliver a song, but he hoped his words would find a responsive target—namely, her heart.

"Hi," he said, ostensibly to the crowd but he could only see one person. "You may be familiar with a dating app called EverAftr—" He waited for the crowd's applause to die down. "Good. I see you've heard of it. When Screenweb approached us about creating a series based on the app, they had a certain pitch in mind—me. Specifically, they wanted me to use the app, alongside six ordinary people from across the United States, all of us searching for a long-term romantic commitment. I guess they thought America would be entertained by watching a boring software engineer like myself try to find someone who'd agree to date him."

The audience laughed again, except for Finley. The color had leeched out of her cheeks. But her gaze remained fixed on him.

"And yes, I'm a believer in EverAftr, the dating app. I created EverAftr when my sisters complained they were having a hard time meeting potential life partners, and somehow I got them to agree to be among EverAftr's beta testers. Now Lauren is married to her husband, Reid, and Claire is married to her wife, Berit. So, when Screenweb approached me with the idea, I thought, why not? I'm also a big believer in happily ever after—the concept, that is."

Finley dropped her gaze. Her head swiveled from left to right, as if she sought the nearest exit.

He hurried on. "Here's the thing, though. I created EverAftr for people who had yet to meet their partner. People hoping that somewhere there was a perfect match for them. And no dating app can promise its users they will find love. Or that they will be with the person they met though the app in one year or ten years. But I stand behind EverAftr's track record of happy customers. Soul mates do exist."

Finley started to back into the crowd behind her, before turning and weaving her way toward the elevator. Any second now, and he would lose sight of her in the sea of people packing the pool deck.

"Which is why I'm *not* a user of the EverAftr app. I was lucky. I found my match a long time ago. But we lost each other until recently."

Finley paused, her back to him so he couldn't see her expression.

"And that got me to thinking. What if EverAftr could be used not only for people who haven't met their partner yet, but also to reunite couples who parted but might want a second chance? I spoke to Screenweb about my idea, and they agreed. So, I'd like to present to you clips from *Finding EverAftr* and its companion series, *Finding EverAftr: The Second Time*. *Finding EverAftr* will debut this summer, and if all goes well, *The Second Time* will come out this fall. Fortunately for the viewers, I will only be on camera as the host."

Finley turned around. She slowly made her way back to standing in front of the stage again.

He smiled at her. Just her. The rest of the crowd melted into multicolored mist. "I may not get my happily-ever-after. Life is complicated. You can want someone but give them up because you think that's best for them. Or maybe the other person doesn't want the same things as you. And I respect that."

Finley remained statue-still. But her dark eyes shimmered in the setting sun.

"But I want her to know I love her. I never stopped, despite trying. I resented how we broke up the first time. I didn't understand the pressures she faced. But since we met again, I hope she knows my thoughts and plans have been with her in mind. She alone is the reason why I'm here on this stage." He took a deep breath, willing Finley to listen, to hear not only with her ears but her heart. "Once upon a time, I didn't fight for her. I didn't convince her she was not only loved, but beloved. But I'm fighting for her now." He put the microphone back on its stand, his gaze never leaving hers, hoping she could read in his eyes what words were too inadequate to express. "You are very much loved, Lee. I love you."

Her hand came up to cover her mouth. Her chest rose and fell under the clinging silk of her dress.

"So." He finally pulled his gaze from Finley and motioned to the nearby technician in charge of running the video. He spoke into the microphone. "Enjoy the sneak peek of *Finding EverAftr.*"

The audience, who had been so silent during his speech he could hear the pool filters hum, broke into boisterous applause and Finley was swallowed by the mass of people pushing toward the stage to shout questions at him. The Screenweb publicist tried to grab his attention. The president of the streaming service, his face wreathed in smiles as he no doubt anticipated the scores of press articles that would be written about Will's speech, held out his hand for a hearty congratulatory handshake. Ji-Hoon, standing by the side of the stage to watch the footage, gave Will two thumbs-up.

Will ignored them all. He strode off the dais. He had one focus: Finley. Ji-Hoon followed him, keeping those who would intercept Will at bay as he parted the crowd, looking for his target.

He found her standing alone in a far corner, her back to him, her face turned to the nearby skyscrapers.

"Lee?" Maybe this had been a bad idea. Maybe a public declaration of love had been the wrong move. But she didn't believe him when it had just been the two of them on the ranch. How better to show her he meant what he said than for his words to be witnessed by hundreds of people, many of whom carried cameras and video recorders? "Are you angry?"

She spun around. Her face was wet with tears. "Of course I'm angry. You made me cry. I never cry." Then she threw her arms around his neck and pulled his mouth to hers. "You realize your speech is about to go viral on every single media platform, don't you?" she whispered against his lips.

"I'm confused. Does that mean you're angry or not?"

She laughed and shook her head. He tears continued to fall. "Only at myself, for breaking up with you twice. What a fool I am."

"Hey, don't talk that way about the woman I love." He smiled and kissed the damp path on her cheeks. "I meant every word."

She sniffled and nodded. "I know. And I'm so sorry, for everything. For the original breakup, for the second breakup, for not trusting you when you said we could find a way forward. Can you forgive me?"

"Always." He smoothed back a lock of her hair. "And you were right to push me on my commitments. I was about to walk away from the contract. That would have been a bad, costly decision."

She smiled, the sparkle in her eyes returning. "Two series, huh? Not a terrible compromise."

"I had to agree to host and reduce the license fee for using EverAftr's name. But they liked the second-chance idea almost better than the original concept. Thanks for being my inspiration."

"Anytime. And thank you for telling Ji-Hoon about the O'Donnell mess. I assume you've heard the news?"

"About the indictments? Yes. Congratulations on being in the clear. I hear your press conference was a bust, however."

She laughed, but then sobered. "I almost screwed that up, too, by not informing Grayson and Nelle about my plan. For so long, I thought I had to arrange everything by myself, or it would all fall apart… And I was good at it. I was a damn good chief of staff and campaign manager."

"I know. Because I know you. You're smart and competent and you care about the people around you."

"But everything became a transaction. There had to be winners and losers. Nothing was freely given. And that was comfortable for me, because that's all I knew." She sighed. "I'm sorry it took me so long to see you were right. I was scared. Of us. Of our future. Of how…big…you make me feel."

"Big?"

"Like I take up space of my own. That I can just… exist, and that's enough. I'm not used to taking up space. I squeeze my way into other people's spaces instead. When I should be letting others in." She shook her head. "I'm not making much sense. You scrambled my brain with that very public speech of yours." She smiled at him, open and genuine. "I'm pretty sure people in Madagascar are watching clips of you speaking right now."

"Let them. And if the clips are wiped off the internet, I'll give the speech all over again on our fiftieth wedding anniversary." He took her chin in his left hand, gazing into the warm brown eyes he adored so much. "You matter, Lee. Not your family, not your job, not even your ability to pull strings and play games to protect the people you love. You. And I love you."

"I love you, so much." She moved to kiss him, but he pulled back, just a half-inch.

"And if a relationship based on an intense experience doesn't work, we can always base the relationship on sex." He grinned at her.

Her eyes widened. "You…you watched the movie *Speed*! You really do love me."

Then her lips were on his and they sank together into the kiss, the lights of Los Angeles swirling around them and creating a shimmering world for two.

Fifteen

One year later

Finley Smythe loved weddings. Especially when they were her own. And especially when they were spur-of-the-moment Las Vegas weddings presided over by an Elvis impersonator. She and Will were second in line, but it would soon be their turn.

"Ready to begin our happily-ever-after?" she asked the groom, handsome in a pair of board shorts topped by a T-shirt that read, "If Lost or Drunk, Return to the Bride." Her own T-shirt read, "I Was Told I'm the Bride."

They were in Las Vegas to attend the country's largest wedding trade show. Both TV series had become so successful, Screenweb had asked for a third. Finley came up with *Finding EverAftr: Saying I Do,* featuring the weddings of couples who united on the previous series, and the streaming service executives jumped at it. Will had bowed out of hosting yet another series—he had an actual company to run, after all—but Screenweb loved Finley's presence on camera. This trip was to tape interstitial footage to be shown between scenes of the couples' weddings.

And when in Vegas…

"You can't believe in that fairy tale," Will said, his expression straight. "You're too smart."

"I have it on very good authority such a thing exists." Finley adjusted the oversized pink tulle bow decorating her hair.

"On whose?"

"On mine. And I'm going to prove it to you, every day." She flung her arms around his neck.

He smiled, laughter and love spilling from his gaze, and pulled her closer. "I think you mean we're going to prove it to each other."

"For ever after."

"And ever after."

* * * * *

*Don't miss a single Titans of Tech novel
by Susannah Erwin!*

Wanted: Billionaire's Wife
Cinderella Unmasked
Who's the Boss Now?
Ever After Exes

Available exclusively from Harlequin Desire.

SPECIAL EXCERPT FROM

⊕ HARLEQUIN

DESIRE

*After the loss of his brother, rancher Nick Hartmann is
suddenly the guardian of his niece. Enter Rose Kelly—
the new tutor. Sparks fly, but with his ranch at stake and
the secrets she's keeping, there's a lot at risk for both...*

Read on for a sneak peek at
Montana Legacy
by Katie Frey.

The ranch was more than a birthright—it was the thing that
made him a Hartmann. His dad made him promise. Maybe
Nick couldn't voice why that promise was important to him.
Why he cared. His brothers shrugged the responsibility so
easily, but he was shackled by it. His legacy couldn't be
losing the thing that had made him. No. He couldn't fail at
this. Not even to be with her, the mermaid incarnate.

She smiled her odd half smile and splashed some water
at him again. "I don't think you even know all you want,
cowboy." She bit her lip, drawing his attention instantly to
the one thing he'd wanted since meeting her at the airport.
He followed her in a second lap of the pool, catching up to
her in the deep end.

"So your brother married your prom date?" She widened
her eyes as she issued her question.

"It was a long time ago." He cleared his throat. Maybe
Ben was right and he needed to open up a bit.

"Yes, you're practically ancient, aren't you?" She swatted
a bit of water in his direction, which he managed to sidestep.

"Careful, Oxford." He smiled, unable to help himself. It felt good to smile, even more so when faced with the crushing sadness he'd been shouldering for the past three weeks.

"Can you not call me that?" She paused. "My sister went to Oxford. And I don't want to think about her right now."

Her bottom lip jutted forward and quivered. It provoked a response he was unprepared for, and he sealed her concern with a kiss so thorough it rocked him.

Everything he wanted to say he said with the kiss. *I'm sorry. I want you. I'm hurting. Let's forget this.* Her body, hot against his, was a welcome heat to balance the chill of the pool. It was soft and deliciously curved. The perfect answer to his desperate question.

His tongue parried hers and she opened to him with an earnestness that rocked him. A soft mew of submission and he lifted her legs around his, arousal pressed plainly against her. She wrapped her legs around him, the thin skin of the bathing suit a poor barrier, and bit gently at his lip.

"I'm sorry," he started.

"Let's not be sorry, not now." Gone was the sorrow. Instead, she looked at him with a burning fire that he matched with his own.

Don't miss what happens next in
Montana Legacy
by Katie Frey.

Available April 2022 wherever
Harlequin Desire books and ebooks are sold.

Harlequin.com

HDEXP0222

Love Harlequin romance?

DISCOVER.

Be the first to find out about promotions, news and exclusive content!

Facebook.com/HarlequinBooks

Twitter.com/HarlequinBooks

Instagram.com/HarlequinBooks

Pinterest.com/HarlequinBooks

YouTube.com/HarlequinBooks

ReaderService.com

EXPLORE.

Sign up for the Harlequin e-newsletter and download a free book from any series at **TryHarlequin.com**

CONNECT.

Join our Harlequin community to share your thoughts and connect with other romance readers!
Facebook.com/groups/HarlequinConnection

HSOCIAL2021